ALECTRYOMANCER
AND OTHER WEIRD TALES
Christopher Slatsky

DUNHAMS MANOR PRESS

Dunwich – East Brunswick – Fisherville

Published by
DUNHAMS MANOR PRESS
67 Dunhams Corner Road
East Brunswick, New Jersey 08816
USA

An imprint of
DYNATOX MINISTRIES
http://dunhamsmanor.com
http://dynatoxministries.com

First Paperback Edition.

Contents

For Andrea, Roman, and August

And an emphatic thank you to Jordan Krall, Paula McAuliffe, Joseph Zanetti, Scott Nicolay, Anya Martin, John Claude Smith, Scott R. Jones, and Matthew Bartlett. You've all been influential whether you know it or not.

LOVELINESS LIKE A SHADOW

The face had spread across a wider section of the wall.

Eleanor's flat possessed an ominous air despite her skepticism towards hauntings, demonic beings, or paranormal nonsense in general. The formation brought to mind the Bélmez Faces, those weird images that appeared on the concrete floor of a house in Spain decades ago. It was unnerving, particularly with all of her sculptures around the flat in various stages of completion. Too many things making eye contact.

She was reminded of her grandmother's stories about *domovoj*, house spirits whose antics ran the gamut from protective to diabolical. Eleanor half expected to catch a glimpse of its white hair and eyes glowing like coals in the middle of the night. But those were old world superstitions.

Just a water stain. Faulty plumbing. Accumulated moisture. When the head first began oozing through the wall's paint Eleanor thought her clay sculptures might be responsible. Maybe mold had survived inside a package of Plastilina clay, oily spores drifting to the walls once she'd started kneading, sculpting, and manipulating the material. When the handyman found a leaky pipe and repaired it she assumed the real culprit had been found.

But that didn't seem to be the case. The flat's plumbing probably went back to the Victorian era—must be another old pipe buried somewhere deep within.

This is what you get for packing it all in, jetting off to London to slum in your art studio. Bohemian lifestyle.

Livin' the expat dream.

The stain was more pronounced this morning. A definite chin, full lips, prominent brow, deep splotches of darkness for eyes, a welter of hair.

One side of the mouth hung lower, a slack-jawed quality that suggested advanced age more than any decreased intellectual capacity. The countenance was gaunt, furrowed cheekbones and a square jaw gave the impression of tight skin over delicate bones.

It bore a vague similarity to her sculptures' faces.

"Seein' shit in clouds that ain't there." Eleanor said. A dismissive attitude did little to lessen her grim mood.

She'd tried to scrub the mess away when it first appeared, but only managed to smear gray sludge across the cream-colored walls. The face was back by that afternoon. So much for getting her tenancy deposit back.

Nothing had gone according to plan. Every attempt to better her life had resulted in something of equal or greater importance being ruined. Why should this be any different?

Nearly a year gone by and Eleanor was still licking her wounds from the divorce. Marriage struck down by "irreconcilable differences" at the ripe old age of 35—she wanted a child, but Joel refused to allow any obstacle to impede his ascension up the corporate ladder. Eleanor certainly didn't feel that a daughter or son was necessary to fulfill her personally, but she resented Joel's emphatic rejection of her wants and desires. He'd made the decision, and though she never had any driving maternal instinct to procreate, her being denied a choice in the matter was the final straw.

So here she was, finally pursuing her own interests and not kowtowing to Joel's whims. No longer concerned she'd spent years supporting him as he pursued his law degree, while she'd deferred art school to an unspecified future date.

But she'd do anything just to have him back. Work the two jobs again, pretend what he did during the day was more important than what she'd suffered through. Have sex on his schedule. Walk on eggshells around his moods. Toil in silence so he could become a better man.

She felt guilty for running away from home to pick up the remaining pieces, giving up any pretense of properly mourning the demise of a 15-year relationship. She'd bummed her first cigarettes from him under the bleachers at the Cottage Hollow homecoming game, saw their first R-rated film together after his friends let them in through the theater exit. Got drunk, shoplifted clothes for the first time with him. She'd married her first love.

It didn't hurt that Joel was gorgeous, even with that wispy attempt at a beard. They'd married young. Her grandparents had spent far too much on that elaborate Russian Orthodox wedding. The newlyweds had such fun with the *vykup nevesty* gifts. Eleanor hadn't laughed that much during all their years together.

All that joy and pain was festering inside like malignant cells. Metastasized memories. Maybe it was time to fly back to the states, back to her condo in Pasadena. Cut her losses.

But she was in the U.K. now, and there was no going back. Not until she came to grips with the fact she was alone. There was some liberation in that. She was here to work on her art. That was the only reason she'd left home. The divorce settlement had made the relocation possible. She wasn't about to give everything up second-guessing herself over a shadow or mold or whatever it was on her wall. She'd come close to throwing in the towel last summer when the unusually muggy weather encouraged the Thames to cough up a particularly nasty insect infestation. Eleanor had no idea why Brits didn't feel the need to install air conditioning or screen doors in every home.

After she'd moved, her U.K. friends did their damndest to cheer her up. Touristy wastes of time, clubs, introducing her to various new age concepts they claimed would alleviate her depression: meditating at Stonehenge, self-actualization techniques, even Wicca. She half-heartedly went through the ritualized motions, but found the concept that she could have any influence on the external world to be so much nonsense. Silly posturing gussied up as profound wisdom.

She had to face the fact that she was never going to get back with her ex. Distancing herself from everything had worked so far. A stone mask of apathy had been beneficial. But she could either be miserable for the rest of her years, or pursue something that made life less of a slog.

A child would have ruined everything, she insisted. But her internal voice wasn't convinced. She wasn't sure if she was undecided due to a sincere desire to raise another human being, or an obstinate opinion derived solely from her wanting to defy Joel in the only way she was capable.

She'd discovered a renewed sense of purpose in her art. A spark of hope there. And it just so happened her freedom was predicated on severing all ties with Joel.

Such were the vagaries of life.

After a week of persistent social network messages, Eleanor finally accepted her friend Lydia's invitation to a gallery showing in Soho. Several artists were scheduled to attend, but Eleanor was mostly looking forward to Vashti's participation.

Vashti was phenomenal.

Eleanor felt a visceral thrill when she'd first explored Vashti's art online. Her sculptures tackled controversial issues—when conception began, how consciousness is predicated on the physical brain encased in a physical head with distinct features. Fetus shaped blobs of clay with adult-sized craniums; faces sculpted from soft earth that gave the objects an ontogenical quality; scalps adorned with flowing manes of real human hair. Sculpture was clearly her calling, her faith, her very purpose. Vashti's creations were designed to confuse and outrage and elicit arguments. And judging by the comments on the site, she'd done that and more.

Eleanor ran her forefinger across the smooth lips of her most recent clay model. Nothing as skilled or interesting as Vashti's work. No comparison. Just another face. She'd no idea whose it was, but this stranger insisted it take form beneath Eleanor's hands every time. Again and again. The clay sank slightly under her touch. Organic. The lack of a pulse seemed a mistake. Self-hardening clay should firm up soon enough.

Someone was crying next door.

Eleanor looked out the flat's only window. Her building was separated by a narrow brick alley, the sole resident a fox living off of leftovers from the bins. The presence of such a creature was endearing, more romantic than the feral opossums and raccoons she encountered back in the U.S. Only two metres separated her window from the window of the other flat. As usual, the tenant's lights were off.

Eleanor had seen the woman a handful of times since she'd moved in, but only during the day, coming and going on her errands.

The flat was always pitch black at night.

She was a tall, graceful, willowy thing. An older woman, though Eleanor had never seen her face without a veil, assuming her age from her posture and the measured, confident way she moved down the street.

There was an elusive, indescribable quality about her—in the vintage yet fashionable clothes she wore, in the luxuriously silver gleam of her healthy hair. Maybe a retired model? An actor who'd decided to spend her remaining years far away from anything resembling wealth or glamour? But the veil and the large demographic of Muslims in Whitechapel made Eleanor consider the religious possibility. But come to think of it, it was unusual she'd only seen the woman with a veil, not a traditional *hijab*.

A candle flame bobbed inside the flat, much to Eleanor's surprise. Flickering like a serpent's burning tongue. This was the first time she'd ever seen any nocturnal presence across the way.

The weeping grew more plaintive, a soul piercing cry that made Eleanor think of the helplessness and despair she felt that moment she was fully aware that Joel was gone from her life.

Or the soul crushing terror from one of her bouts of sleep paralysis. The disorder had recently returned, reinvigorated by the increased stress in her life.

She was about 5 when she'd first experienced it. Sleeping on the bottom bunk, her older sister snoring up top. A thin naked woman had settled on her chest, a coiled weight, loose skin slopping over her ribs onto the floor. Wild confusion of hair trembling in the air like shock lines around a comic strip character's head. A stunningly beautiful face. Mask of someone else's mask. All that hair whipping and hissing with blind aggression.

And Eleanor unable to move a muscle. A slab of breathing marble.

But she was an adult now and no longer feared any nocturnal visitations. She understood the physiology of sleep disorders, knew that it was a biological thing. Explainable. Not a strange entity visiting from some nameless place. Xanax would keep the phantom entity at bay.

She held her breath to better hear the cries from the other flat, but just as quickly as it had started, the weeping was silenced.

Eleanor had lunch with Lydia, then swung by Sainsbury's on the way back home. She was glad to be in and out of the grocery store quickly; the place was a crowded madhouse. A sea of faces all blending together into a uniform expression of dumbfounded petulance and irrational rage. Cold granite, moronic countenances.

Her shopping trolley was jostled by the tiniest of obstacles on the rutted sidewalk. Grocery bags rustled, glass clinked. London's aging infrastructure was often in the back of her mind, as was the recent spate of exploding pavement—a consequence of worn electrical cables bursting underground when it rained. All those kilometers of passages down there to facilitate the sewage systems running into Battersea for processing. So many transportation tunnels allowed countless possibilities for disaster underfoot.

The mysterious neighbor's front door was ajar.

She must be home then. Hadn't Eleanor been living here long enough for introductions? Sure, Londoners *were* more private than tourists from the states, and Eleanor risked stepping over politeness into ugly American territory, but it *would be* rude of her not to officially greet a neighbor.

She left her trolley on the sidewalk and knocked on the door.

Nobody answered. She tilted her head to the door's gap. Nothing. No voices or footsteps, no sound or movement whatsoever.

"Hello? I'm your neighbor. Eleanor. You left your door open."

Silence.

Eleanor entered the dim flat. It was completely unfurnished. No pictures on the walls, no gewgaws adorning the windowsill where she could see into her own home a metre away. She felt as if she were retracing her steps, going back over ground already covered. But that couldn't be the case. She'd never been in this flat before.

She opened one of the two closed doors. It was a bathroom. No toiletries or towels. Even the toilet paper dispenser was empty. She closed the door and went to investigate the other room.

The wood floor creaked in protest when she stepped inside.

The ceiling was high and narrow, the room longer than expected. A tall, thin window at the end allowed enough gray light to enter for Eleanor to see that the walls were decorated with various shades of small oval patterns. Wallpaper even covered the ceiling.

A train rattled by on the Hammersmith line, its lights brightening the room briefly. The wall's ovals had blond and black hair. Some wore glasses.

The wallpaper wasn't decorative.

Thousands of photo booth snaps and passport pictures. Just the faces stapled and glued to every available surface. Strangers looking down, frozen like stone busts in an abandoned gallery. They even covered the back of the door. Eleanor instinctually averted her gaze from the cut out heads.

A small box sat in the corner of the room. She'd known the box would be there. But that couldn't be. There was no way she could have known.

She removed the lid. It was filled with mutilated photos, driving licenses, passports from various countries. She stuck her fingers inside, moved the clipped papers and bits of plastic around.

There was something at the bottom. She pulled out a journal, then another. Some with burgundy faux leather covers, others black and tan or shiny red plastic. She riffled through one. It was in French. Another in Japanese. She was quickly becoming uncomfortable with all of this. She placed them back in the box, at the bottom, beneath everything. On a whim she reached back in and withdrew a glossy mauve journal. She opened it to a random page.

4/11

I write this knowing that if you haven't already had a butchers at what's hanging from the attic's rafters, you will soon enough. I can only imagine your expression—maybe a spot of exasperation at not being able to identify just what it is, mingled with curiosity over how something that size managed to crawl all the way up there.

I know you're all impatient chivvy along types, and I've refrained from complaining about that particular trait over the years. I'll keep this brief. It's time to burn bridges and I mean to do so in a spectacular fashion. I do intend to let the cat out of the bag.

Well, not a cat exactly is it?

Eleanor heard sobbing.

The exhausted, hopeless cry of someone who'd lost everything that mattered. Hysterical yet constrained gasps that spoke of death and love. Something in the voice gave acknowledgement to the fact that nothing in life was worthwhile, cowardice the only reason they continued living. Eleanor had heard her own voice sound so very similar, on far too many occasions, since leaving her home and family.

She closed the journal. Buried it with the others.

She was certain the sound was coming from beneath her feet. She looked to the center of the room. The bare wood floor here was scuffed and deeply scratched. Hinges and a metal handle stood out in stark contrast to the dark wood.

The old woman slipped through this hatch. There's a tunnel down there that connects to all of the other hidey-holes in London. Why the fuck not?

Eleanor tugged at the handle. The trapdoor was locked from below. Whoever was down there must be able to get out on their own then. She felt a bit relieved at this revelation.

The smell hit her. A reptilian musk. Rotting meat. Like a poorly maintained vivarium.

The old woman moves about freely down there. Unnoticed. In secret.

The wailing increased in volume, though the tone was different now, a raw uninhibited quality to its fervor.

The hungry cry of a newborn baby.

Eleanor stepped back. Should she call out to make sure everything was ok? Ring the police? She backed out of the room. Abrupt, hurried steps led her to the entrance. She left the front door in the same position she'd found it. None of this was any of her business. She'd gone poking her nose in where she shouldn't have. Best to leave well enough alone.

All of her actions were familiar, like an old videotape recorded over long forgotten shows, fleeting images of the original programming peeking through.

It had started to rain while she was inside. Thick, oily drops clung to everything. She rolled her grocery cart back to her flat, the soggy contents of the bags sloshing as the wheels caught every crack and bump in the sidewalk.

When she arrived home she closed the blinds so she wouldn't have to see the neighbor's flat.

The pattern had acquired Eleanor's distinct chin and subtle shape of her forehead, yet retained the sunken black blemishes where eyes should be. It looked as if it had been intentionally sketched by a child with charcoal powdered hands, slapping their palms against the wall, wiping shadows across the surface. A trickle of moisture had further distorted the visage, lengthening it into a wedge shape not unlike a snake's head. The hair was vibrant, growing further up the wall and across the ceiling.

Eleanor wasn't staring at her own face. She was seeing things that simply weren't there, convincing herself that the water-stain hair was undulating with supple life. She'd been rash enough to enter a stranger's home—she simply didn't have her head screwed on right at the moment. Everything was coming across as threatening due to stress.

She took a sip of Merlot from a juice glass, the daffodil design circling the base faded and chipped. A dark flake floated in the pink liquid. She let her mouthful trickle back into the glass, set it on the knife gouged Formica counter. There was some currant squash in the small refrigerator, but the thought of drinking the beverage weak left a cloyingly sweet memory in her mouth.

Lydia had texted a reminder that the art exhibit was that evening, so Eleanor had started on a new sculpture to get into the artistic mood of things.

But this one looked like all the others. Same dull expression. Same features. She no longer felt she was an artist, more like a forensic anthropologist sculpting a corpse's visage from the remnants of a former life, resurrecting an identity lost to violence and decay. She'd tried to make a simple object, a bowl, a vase, anything except an anthropomorphic representation. But every time she manipulated a blob of clay it demanded it take the shape of the head she'd become all too familiar with.

She set her tools aside, pushed the modeling stand away in frustration. The wheels squeaked until it gently came to rest against the wall.

A walk around the neighborhood would put her in a better frame of mind. Fresh air, would do wonders. Best to have a clear head before visiting the gallery tonight.

The rain tapped her umbrella like impatient fingertips. She kept her head down, walking quickly, the need to stretch her legs and fill her lungs with untainted air more important than being aware of her surroundings. She only looked up briefly when passing the mysterious woman's flat. The door was closed.

She walked with a frenetic pace until she'd reached Shoreditch and the bustling crowds.

Her umbrella scraped against a body. Eleanor turned to offer an apology. The businessman kept going, seemingly unaware of the intrusion. The drizzle and a fog of cigarette smoke thick around his shoulders made it appear as if his head was a lump of malleable clay, glistening with the silvery sheen of connective tissue.

Eleanor nervously walked against the milling masses, down the stairs into the tube station. Her right foot slipped on the slick pavement. She waved her Oyster card over the reader, walked through the gate. She closed her umbrella, head low with determination, dreading eye contact with any stranger. She didn't know why this was of such concern, but the fear was so palpable she didn't even look up after roughly bumping against someone exiting the train.

She stood inside the packed car, one hand holding a rail, the other gripping her umbrella as if it were a weapon. Passengers swayed listlessly as the train roared through dark tunnels. The lights grew dim, darkened, lit the interior again. Eleanor had the sense that people's faces were jumping about every time the lights flickered, sliding from person to person, swapping identities. A bearded young man's taciturn expression took the place of a woman wearing a headscarf who swapped the frown of a heavyset woman talking on her mobile who exchanged—

The train's announcer bellowed the name of the next stop, snapping Eleanor out of her daydream. The car slowed. Before the doors even slid open, Eleanor pushed her way to the front of the exiting passengers. She ran up the stairs to the surface. The bustling crowd moved in an unnatural manner, as if they were extras in a film that was so low budget they had to use the same faces over and over again.

In her haste, she jostled an elderly woman. She stumbled to the ground despite Eleanor's desperate attempt to slow her fall. Mortified, she moved to help her up.

It must have been the adjacent fish and chip shop's blue-green florescent lights molding the woman's waxen forehead, cheeks and mouth into something soft. The gray hair uncoiling from her bun only accentuated the impression her skull was indented where she'd pressed up against the cashpoint machine.

The woman raised her runny face and croaked a word that sounded more like a tarry bubble bursting than a coherent phrase.

Eleanor apologized profusely, but the old woman didn't respond. She regained her composure, wobbled to her feet, moved along. The dull, acne pocked face of the chip-shop's cashier stared at her from behind the window. A hazy oval, like a splotch of grease.

A panic attack. What else could account for the commuters changing into a stone-headed mob before her eyes? What other reason could there be for their faces congealing into stony visages?

Frozen mono-identities, manufactured statues. An assembly line of us all.

Anxiety and an artist's imagination. Guilt over trespassing and snooping in an old woman's home. That explained everything.

Everything.

Eleanor opened her umbrella and walked back to her flat as fast as she could on the slick pavement without risking a fall.

"The Shroud of Turin does not portray the face of Christ." The short man stood just inches away from the tapestry. An unnamed artist had screen-printed the infamous image onto a sheet of denim, presumably as an anti-consumerist statement. "Don't misunderstand, it is an *acheiropoieton*, but we are not gazing upon the visage of our Lord and Savior. The Turin cloak boasts the face of a demon."

Eleanor gave a wry smile in acknowledgement. The strange man was a squat stack of a human being. He was perspiring heavily. Lydia was nowhere to be found. She was growing more and more concerned that her friend had yet to respond to any text messages.

Nothing but strangers here. Eleanor couldn't retain the distinctive features of individuals in her memory. It was as if she'd been afflicted with a spontaneous case of prosopagnosia.

"You're familiar with the Shroud?" the short man asked without removing his gaze from Christ's bloodied face. Thick glasses made the man's eyes almost comically large.

"I'm familiar. *Not made by hands*. I don't think the real shroud is miraculous or anything. It's a medieval painting." Eleanor scanned the room, hoping she'd be able to place Lydia's pretty smile in the crowd.

"So is this art? Or sacrilege?" The little man waved his hand at the denim shroud as if offended.

Eleanor raised glass to lips to hide her smile. "Art. Then again, I think Marcel Duchamp was onto something."

"Oh. So you do—"

Eleanor didn't hear the rest.

A wave of déjà vu enveloped her. She didn't belong here. This conversation had happened before, everything all too recognizable. She wasn't standing in an art gallery holding a wine glass. She was in her flat holding a chipped juice glass and staring at something she couldn't quite recall.

No, she could smell the short man's cheap cologne. Feel the cool London air slip through an open window. Hear the pretentious conversations.

And she could see Vashti herself.

Vashti was striking. A tall, lithe woman in a tailored dark green suit. The lower half of her face was obscured by a red veil. She moved like a memory, effortless, yet not in a distinct enough manner to describe. That veil, her posture, the graceful way she greeted the guests, all seemed as if Eleanor had experienced this before.

She watched Vashti scrutinize the crowd. The sculptress' perfectly shaped face refused to be fully hidden by her veil. Flawless skin meant whatever age her voice and body language suggested, her complexion reduced the years considerably. Straight silver hair fell to her waist. She was beauty and artistic genius personified.

Eleanor was certain she'd seen her before, and recently at that. They'd been close at some point. Had she passed her in the tube station?

Vashti's eyes conveyed such an intense beauty Eleanor had to consciously keep herself from stepping back. Vashti stood near her sculptures. Eleanor walked over.

A glass fell, shattered against the floor.

Laughter.

Eleanor casually lowered her gaze down to a rock object. It looked like a fossilized internal organ.

Vashti touched her arm.

The corners of Vashti's dark eyes wrinkled at an unseen smile. She leaned in close to Eleanor. Her veil rippled, "Imagine we're all templates of one personality. Everything we are, everything that makes us what we are?" She clicked her tongue against the roof of her mouth. "Simply the slight tweak of the predetermined. All set in stone."

Eleanor didn't know how to respond. She said the first thing that came to mind, "I love your sculptures. They're beautiful."

"You're too kind. You like this one?" Vashti laid her long hand on the organic rock.

"It's remarkable."

"It's mine," Vashti said.

"I came here to see your work specifically."

"No. I mean this is *mine*."

Eleanor was confused. "Yes?"

The sculptures seemed restless. Shadows teased.

Eleanor's hands were hard with dried clay and the bust before her was shaped into something so terrible she never imagined she was capable of sculpting such a thing. She needed a drink, but her glass of wine had something dark floating in it and there was squash in the small fridge but it didn't sound appealing. Someone was sobbing outside her flat's window.

She was mistaken. She was in the gallery, conversing with Vashti. She looked at the sculpture. It was labeled **LITHOPEDION XXIV**.

"It's mine." Vashti whispered. "All of them are mine.*"

The gallery filled with the musk of snakes deep underground.

This had all already happened.

Eleanor thanked Vashti, excused herself, turned towards the exit.

A newborn screamed.

Eleanor was back in her flat, staring at the smudge of face on her wall.

She wasn't sure how she came to be here. Some internal clock told her hours had passed, or perhaps hours had yet to pass. She remembered heads teetering like hardened clay busts on rickety armatures. Calcified hands losing their grip on wine glasses.

Guests toppling, shattering into powdery segments on the floor.

The ominous possibility that she hadn't left the flat in weeks, if not months, slithered at the back of her brain. This thought was distant, hysterical delirium, a miasma of divine dreaming. An omnipresent gaze locked on the never-ending gaze that stared the world frozen. Eleanor was so tired, her limbs unnaturally heavy. Where was Lydia?

She could hear what she hoped was the fox rummaging around in the dustbin in the alley. She knew it wasn't her old furry friend. The sound wasn't delicate enough; it was the raucous noise a heavy body makes undulating across the ground.

And that incessant crying, that damned crying, so sorrowful, omnipresent, as if it would be there even after death.

How long had she been here in her flat? Why was she so thin? Why was she *ravenous*? She'd closed the blinds when she'd left earlier. Someone had opened them.

No, the blinds had been removed and lay in a crumple on the floor.

She was mistaken. The window was gone.

A gaping hole connected her flat to the alleyway to the neighbor's sparse flat and the drapes were coiling around and over themselves in humps forming a torso that rose and tapered into a terrible yet delicate face perched daintily up top like an obscene ornament.

The face was no longer wearing a veil. She spoke in a lovely voice, *I am the sorrow in beauty.*

Eleanor didn't have to glance at her sculptures to know that they all wore her own countenance. She looked to the face-stain on the wall. It was as if she were looking into a mirror. *All I ever dreamed of was to be the one to determine how to attain happiness.*

She inhaled before her lungs were fully ossified, exhaled before her body became too stiff to speak,

"If my heart turns to stone, I won't feel it shatter."

She managed a wan smile.

The stain smiled back.

AN INFESTATION OF STARS

When Lilly opened the colorfully wrapped parcel she thought it was a unique edition of the New Testament—of what version she was uncertain for the spindly messiah on the cover was unlike any painting of Christ she'd ever seen. The artist portrayed the crucifix's wood as ravaged by tunneling and flanked by weird cherubs with rotund bellies, a multitude of growths sprouting from their ankles, concluding at the nape of their necks in imitation of wings. The protuberances reminded Lilly of a species of lichen that grew on the bottom of decayed tree limbs she'd turn over in the woods in hopes of finding interesting bugs.

"Happy birthday, sweetheart. Hope you like it."

"Thank you, momma. Papa. It's beautiful."

Lilly's mother and father traveled the world studying various cultures amongst strange and wondrous corners of the Earth—she was a sickly thing afflicted with a neurological disorder that confined her to moving about with a crutch.

They'd spent most of their careers collecting data on a religious sect who'd dubbed themselves the *Drachtig*, even going so far as to relocate to the cult's isolated compound near the Pontoetoe village. Here they focused their anthropological research on the *Drachtig's* elaborate rituals, most of which were inspired by their reverence of insects.

As such, Lilly's parent's souvenirs of icons in the shape of grotesque bug-gods never struck her as odd. And while their gift of a Bible that year *was* somewhat predictable, its contents were quite unusual.

The book's interior was embellished with art representing various world's faiths, many of which Lilly didn't recognize. The pictures ran the gamut from traditional Christian images—one appeared to be from a hand block print depicting Mary and Child, their eyes scarlet pools of kermes dye—another a *suiboku* painting of the Buddha under a Bhodi tree.

His abdomen was strangely articulated.

There were more abstract works as well, with colors swirling like the convoluted whorls and cells of a subterranean nest. Lilly spent hours holding a magnifying glass to the pages, revealing details that seemed impossible to apply without some mechanical assistance; the human eye simply could not see such vivid detail unaided. Every page was exquisite, every work of art within overwhelmingly detailed.

The book had no publishing information or interior text whatsoever.

Lilly obsessed over one particular painting depicting two of those disturbing cherubs from the cover rolling a stone away from a tomb opening. There was an insinuation of movement within, a subtle effect of contrasting light suggesting agitation in the pitch black interior. When she held her magnifying glass over the cave's opening it seemed not one entity within but a seething mass.

That painting haunted her sleep.

Lilly's father died under mysterious circumstances shortly after her birthday. There was no autopsy and his cremation guaranteed that the cause of death remain unexplained. Lilly was convinced that his murder (for she was certain his demise had been at the hands of the *Drachtig*) and the book were linked, though she searched its pages in vain for any definitive proof.

Her mother was inconsolable. She took to long walks or reading anthropology publications in privacy.

It was an easy matter for Lilly to freely search her father's study. She rummaged through his desk and found several correspondences her mother had exchanged with anthropologist colleagues.

These missives explained that the body had been mutilated. The locals suspected he'd expired from the lethal bites of the *Paraponera clavata*. Lilly was a clever child and found this quite strange; while that species of ant bite *was* excruciatingly painful, these particular insects were not known to disfigure their prey.

She searched the drawers thoroughly for more documents and found a crumpled carbon copy dated June 14th, five years prior. The carbon impression was faded, her father's handwriting hurried so much of the page was difficult to read. One particular section caught her eye:

...bite of the bullet ant in much the same manner as the Satere-Mawe in coming of age rituals though the [illegible] henosis by the pain invoked. Sta[illegible] omnipresent creature is inherently mindless as consciousness presupposes the ability to distinguish one's self from external objects, but a mind that occupies the entirety of existence can not be both independent from objects in the material world and omnipresent. The emic analysis of extraterrestrial cultures necessitates the acceptance of holometabolous gnosis on ascending [illegible]

When confronted with the letters, Lilly's mother refused to comment and never spoke a word about her husband's death.

Lilly was convinced the journal page was a catalyst for the dreams that began to harass her.

One persistent night terror seemed to be a harbinger of sorts: she'd be standing barefoot, crutch half buried in dirt, the ground scooped out as if an animal had been tunneling beneath her. The earth moist and molasses colored, unimaginable depths descending into stinking wetness like the inside-out viscera of an enormous beast.

There were subtle variations, but the dream inevitably rose to a fever pitch when the icons and figurines her parents had given her over the years crawled from the dirt. Their surfaces glistened sticky red as an oddly configured face tapped its mouth against her bedroom window.

She was certain the dreams were at the very least her subconscious providing clues to her father's death; at best, her father's soul contacting her slumbering mind.

She decided to attempt an experiment, as she was confident that this was what her parents would have done. Late one night, she placed a saucer of honey on the window sill and left the pane open a few inches to allow the outside access at its own volition. She waited for what seemed like hours, the bowl of honey glowing in the lambent star light like a beacon.

The gentle splash of moisture dripping from an overhanging

branch and the patter of some nocturnal animal lulled her into a shallow sleep.

She was abruptly awakened by a repetitive brushing sound. She heard a clump of hirsute stuff rolling back and forth across a surface.

"Hello?" she said, hoping there'd be no response.

She stared at the ceiling where the noise originated. Her pupils contracted to detect a stain writhing in the corner. The stain detached itself from the clinging shadows and quivered above her bed. It spun in place, as if it were being wrapped in a cocoon, far too many thin limbs flailing in a futile attempt to free its swollen body.

Lilly slipped deeper into sleep, unsure whether the thing was confined to dream or the waking realm.

When she woke, she limped to the window to find the bowl was empty and fragmented into porcelain splinters. No honey shone wetly on the sill, no trace of the animal that had consumed the offering.

A profound dread prevented her from passing her hand through the window's opening into the night air. The possibility that her limbs could exceed the confines of her room thrilled her—the same sensation she had when reaching under a crumbling log and blindly grasping at the life squirming underneath.

She carefully picked up the bowl to avoid cutting herself and hid the pieces in a nightstand drawer.

As Lilly grew older her dreams persisted, though a regime of medications made rest bearable. Much of her childhood anxiety now seemed either quaint or simply false memories exaggerated by a nervous disposition. Her nightmares became less threatening, until they too were eventually dismissed as a child's reaction to grief over her father's death.

She attended university at the Universidade de São Paulo and graduated with several anthropology degrees. She found it difficult to completely hide her disappointment over the fact that her disability hampered her ability to freely travel, much less wholly immerse herself in a foreign land. She would never be the globetrotting scientist her parents had been, but made due by diligently pursuing her research in the finest of libraries or her own well stocked study. But frustration and self-loathing were always present, companions that persisted in reminding her of her failures.

When her mother died, Lilly was content that her last days were pleasant, though her paranoia did increase in proportion to her failing health. During the final days she insisted she was being watched by something on the bedroom ceiling.

Lilly studied the *Drachtig*, researching their faith in the hope she'd unveil some secrets from the artwork within her book. She'd grown to love their culture, to admire their profound religious ideologies and social structure. They were not a threatening alien thing, but a fascinating, kind and giving people she no longer believed had a hand in her father's death. Colonialist propaganda had painted them in a cruel, false light.

She interviewed colleagues, spoke with art historians and utilized her extensive scholarly resources to scrutinize the book further. The *Drachtig* themselves had little to offer on the book's origins.

It was all to no avail. All of her efforts simply confirmed that she owned the only known copy of the tome and none of the artists' identities could be determined.

Then one oppressively humid afternoon she was contacted by a Rev. Balim Zuchmog, Th.D.

Having heard of Lilly's interest in the book through her peers at the university, Rev. Zuchmog offered her prodigious knowledge of religious literature to further Lilly's inquiries. They met in the reverend's office and discussed research over coffee.

"I recognize the image of the cherubs moving the boulder from the tomb's opening: it's a detail from an obscure 17th century pamphlet. The *Dolichovespula magna*. Only one surviving fragment exists." Reverend Zuchmog spoke softly as she tenderly turned the book's pages.

This was the first clue Lilly had ever acquired.

The two quickly became close friends. They spent most of their free time drinking from the reverend's rare wine collection, discussing art, religions, occult philosophies.

Though the reverend's degrees were in Oriental studies (she was an expert on religious literature recorded in Old Persian and Avestan), she also held several history and art credentials. Despite her title she was an outspoken atheist and the two spent hours in friendly debate. They enjoyed each other's company. Rev. Zuchmog seemed as excited as Lilly to unlock the book's mysterious roots.

Nearly a year passed and they'd yet to uncover any further information. Lilly was worried that she was once again at a standstill. When Rev. Zuchmog made a request to join her in a scholarly assembly she held annually at her pastorium, Lilly was hesitant; she found the invitation odd as she and the reverend were adept in very different fields. But she explained that Lilly could use the occasion as a think tank in which to seek answers, to brainstorm with theological experts. Lilly agreed to make an appearance.

Reverend Zuchmog insisted she bring the book.

Lilly drove down a winding country lane to a large Federal style brick home set back in the woods. She was punctual, yet there were several vehicles already parked. When Rev. Zuchmog answered the door there were no other guests behind her, no voices from anywhere in the house, much less the familiar clink of ice against glass that normally accompanied such a gathering.

"Where have the guests gone hiding?" Lilly asked.

The reverend smiled. "They're all present and accounted for, but preparing for the business of the evening elsewhere."

This alleviated Lilly's discomfort somewhat, though something troublesome continued to buzz at the back of her mind. They drank and chatted while she habitually riffled through her book and commented on the various artifacts displayed about the home.

After finishing a second drink Lilly heard a bell chime. Rev. Zuchmog hurriedly placed her glass down on a bookshelf and touched Lilly's elbow to escort her to another room. With no explanation offered she handed Lilly a dark brown garment.

"Please. Put this on."

Lilly stood baffled, the garment draped over her forearm, as she watched the reverend slip on a matching robe. She pulled a thin sac cloth over her head, then secured the whole thing around her neck with a frayed cord.

"Care to tell me what's going on here?" Lilly asked.

The reverend shook her head with such a comically solemn demeanor Lilly had to stifle a smile. She felt as if she were being peer pressured to perform some ridiculous college hazing ritual. She followed the reverend's lead and slipped the robe and sac cloth on. A long dormant sense of excitement swept over her.

She wondered if she were joining some secret society of scholars and researchers. The thought seemed ridiculous and juvenile, yet tantalizingly adventurous, like something her parents would have done. The reverend would only respond to her questions with a barely perceptible shake of her head behind the netting.

Lilly followed her down a narrow brick lined corridor, crutch tapping loudly along the way. They stopped at a steel door, its surface stained a green hue like tarnished copper, pock-marked with what appeared to be chemical burns. The reverend produced a key and unlocked the door.

They stepped into a large brightly lit area where dozens of guests strolled about exchanging pleasantries. It was sickeningly warm. The wool robe absorbed the moist air and trapped it against Lilly's skin. She was afraid her sweaty hands would stain her book's cover.

Those in attendance were all wearing the same brown robes, but a few also sported elbow length rubber gloves. Some disguised their faces with ornate masks that gleamed like hardened wax under the hot lights. Lilly couldn't imagine they'd be comfortable in the stifling heat.

The masks were inexplicably terrifying.

Lilly convinced herself she'd joined a social club where the more eccentric members hid their identities to protect their business and community status. The attire was simply a way to identify with a new social group, like a secret handshake or password. While still uncertain about the masked guests, she was gradually becoming more relaxed.

"Drink?" A masked server balanced a tray of cocktails. Each glass held a long thin straw.

She gratefully took one, thanked him, raised the glass to her lips, and then realized what the straws were for. They were thin enough to slip between the holes in the netting over her face.

By Lilly's fourth drink she was conversing freely with her new acquaintances. By her seventh, the conscious world blurred with dream.

But those masks were unsettling.

They accentuated the length of the wearer's jaws in a grotesque manner. There was something in the way the guest's rubber clad fingers squeaked over the straws in their glasses and how they tilted their heads when talking that Lilly found deeply worrisome.

Reverend Zuchmog rang a bell at the front of the room and called for everyone's attention. The crowd quieted and focused on her.

"I am grateful that all of you were able to attend this evening."

In Lilly's inebriated state she heard the voice as a monotone interjected with glottal clicks. The reverend said something about a "hive of stars", followed by witticisms that, judging by the polite laughter, made sense only to those who shared her most recent studies.

When the reverend paused her speech, the crowd filled the silences with a similar whirring gibberish, mouths scarcely moving, thin arms vibrating near their torsos in an unusual manner. It seemed as if the gestures were amplifying their voices. Lilly assumed it must be a product of the room's unusual acoustics. She was drunk. Her brain wasn't deciphering the chanting properly.

Her head was swimming against a tide.

She stumbled towards the exit but the flock kept jostling her, impeding her way to the door. The bright lights and the mesh over her eyes made it difficult to see properly.

Her body felt scorched as panic flushed her skin.

"Excuse me. Excuse me. I don't feel well. Excuse me."

They set their hands on her.

She lashed out with her crutch at anything that loomed close, cracked open any long-jawed face that pressed against her. When her improvised weapon was torn from her grasp she struck out wildly with her fists until her knuckles split. Her hands ran warm and wet.

Lilly released all of her pent up anger at failing to solve her father's murder, her grief over her mother's death, her inability to decipher the book—it all boiled over into a frenzied rage.

Her blows shattered masks. Their texture was unpleasantly brittle, the victims fell back with a hiss. Abnormally contorted hands slapped against their own cheeks and foreheads as if offended at the revealed flesh. The exposed faces had too many eyes, their skin was too smooth, as if painted with a thick sheen of makeup under the masks. In the pulsing light it appeared that the participants she'd wounded were shedding their robes.

The lights flashed brighter, the room saturated with a sodden heat. The alcohol in her blood and the rising temperature furthered her delirium. Mouths spread far too wide from stretched chins. The room trembled with the sound of thousands of knives sharpened on whetstones simultaneously.

In the chaos Lilly didn't know when or where she dropped her book.

Rev. Zuchmog's chant rose to a shriek, her face aglow from something writhing beneath the surface. The flock danced exuberantly, capering about the room, leaping high into the air until their heads bumped against the ceiling.

Bodies flitted against the walls, weightless things that slipped through an open window. Lilly knew it had to be the dancer's shadows floating, and the heaps left behind on the floor must have been people. A vestige of her mind clung to a rational explanation, insisted the mounds that glowed like silk in the weird light were discarded clothes.

She couldn't fathom why the clothes were screaming.

She stumbled to the open window, closed and latched it though she knew it wouldn't prevent anything from re-entering the house. The stars reminded her of larvae twinkling with various shades of intensity. Except they moved incorrectly, puffy bright bodies frantically searching for a place to hide in the soil black night. She rested her burning forehead against the window's cool glass and whispered over and over that she was still asleep, still a little girl dreaming of living stars, and any moment now, her parents would call her name and wake her.

Lilly ran to the front door, past a crutch in the corner, its surface pitted as if from acid burns. She was surprised at how strong her legs had become; even as a child she'd never been able to move this quickly. She accidentally kicked an object that skidded across the floor. She grabbed it, rejoiced in her book's familiar heft and glossy sheen of the cover. When she touched the paper she realized what she'd failed to notice after several decades of analyzing the art within.

The pages had the texture of an insect's paper nest.

She'd suspected this all these years, though her mind had suppressed the truth. She'd obstinately refused to accept the identity of the entities responsible for the book's art. She could no longer doubt.

The *Drachtig* sect had shown her father that existence was indisputably horrific—not a thinking horror that plots behind a vast curtain, but a universe of witless shadow breathing against the thin cells of reality. A cosmos guided solely by self perpetuation unburdened by conscience.

An existence governed by insect morality.

The germ of this truth had been planted in Lilly's head as a child, but had failed to hatch into a full revelation until that very moment. Resigned, she stepped outside to look into the star-clogged sky.

She felt so very healthy, so wonderfully young and strong and confident again. She couldn't restrain her laughter or refuse the joy in her heart.

She flexed her healthy legs, ascended, tore through a gossamer membrane that enveloped creation.

The illimitable squeezed through nighttime windows, gently brushed against sleeping minds, pressed against the world. She held the book tightly against her chest and thought of her parents, her sole regret they had not survived long enough to witness her grand excursion.

"I can see everything now. I can explore everywhere," she said. Ice formed on her eyelashes, the chill of space made her limbs ache.

Existence pullulated with brutish idiocy, teemed with an insect's mindless hunger. The chitinous stars trilled a chorus as Lilly rose, their relentless bites and stings an epiphany of agony and salvation.

They swarmed around Lilly's corpse in celebration.

CORPORAUTOLYSIS

Business Day 1

William returned to work far too soon. He walked down the familiar hallway past the empty cubicles, past a cluster of whispering employees. "...found in the runoff... the Factory." Their voices trailed off as he walked past. "...pretty bad shape I hear." He caught fragments of their conversation despite their attempts at disguising the gossip. "...things grow out there in the muck."

He didn't recognize any of them. They were all fresh faces discussing his life as if they'd known who he was or understood what had happened. He'd survived the tragedy and the last three months by immersing himself in apathy; it made him invulnerable and the days bearable. Gossiping co-workers were irrelevant. He didn't acknowledge their presence but idly rattled his keys in his pocket as he walked by.

Time had not been kind to the Corporation. The building had always been in disrepair but the current degree of dilapidation was shocking. The quaint art collection of children's handprints and bright yellow suns over green landscapes had been removed and replaced by curiously configured water stains. The ceiling tiles were buckled, spotted with smears of gray where maintenance had attempted to scrub the mold away. Several tiles were missing and the gaps were plugged with wads of something bulbous and pale, like an organic brand of environmentally friendly insulation. The once mauve carpet was now faded and worn and there were threadbare rugs laid out to cover what he assumed to be even more offensive stains. Apparently the lawsuits had taken their toll on the building's aesthetics.

William walked quickly towards his desk with the intent of dropping off his keys and heading to the break room for a drink of water. The lights were dimmed, several of the fluorescents turned off or burnt out. He passed by a handwritten note pinned to the department announcement board:

In an effort to save the environmint management has implimented several energee saving measures. Thank you for your cooperasion.

His cubicle had been relatively untouched during his bereavement leave. There was only a small stack of new paperwork and a single envelope on the keyboard. He felt a thin greasy film across the desktop, like furniture polish that hadn't been adequately wiped away. He traced his finger across the surface and though he couldn't see any residue he did detect the earthy scent of mildew.

The front of the envelope read *Welcome Back William*. The contents felt strangely bulky and thick. The card inside had an odd texture as if it were patched together from several layers of parchment. The black, blue and red ink had soaked into the porous paper, creating thick arteries of purple that obscured the messages inside. He squinted, pushed his glasses to the bridge of his nose to focus his vision. He couldn't decipher who had written their well-wishes; the scrawled platitudes were indecipherable. He suspected one delicately written message was the handwriting of the analyst he'd trained just before leaving. He tried to remember her face but it was indistinct, preserved in his mind as a smooth oval with smudged depressions for eyes and a wide stain of a mouth. Pressure swelled in his chest, pinpricks in his brain made him see flashing lights. It was difficult to recall names and he was frustrated at the lack of faces to attach to the missing names.

He glanced down the hall and saw a stack of boxes and filing cabinets blocking the aisle, toppled in a heap like a hastily constructed barricade. This bothered him for the rest of his shift. It was an uncomfortable weight in his head on the drive home.

Business Day 2

"Hey, welcome back." Jensen's head peeked over the cubicle wall and his hand offered a breath mint. "You back for good, buddy?" The illusion of his hand hovering below his unattached head was discomfiting in the dim light.

"Hey. Thanks, Jensen. I am back for good. I'm surviving. Thanks." William took the proffered breath mint and smiled in return. The mint was the same color and shape as his wife's sleeping pills so he just let it roll around on his palm in a closed fist. William liked Jensen, but his voice seemed different, his eyes a different shade of gray and his face puffier than he remembered.

"You look tired, buddy. Fresh coffee in the breakroom. I just put on a pot." Jensen didn't seem to notice when someone coughed far too loudly several cubicles to his right, theatrically, as if on cue.

"Look, Will." Jensen's voice lowered conspiratorially. "You ever need anything, say like to talk or something, just let me know. I'll be a cubicle away, neighbor." He seemed uncomfortable with his magnanimity and played it off with a wink. "This McKinnon lawsuit is killing me. Too much work, not enough time in the day. Well, back to the tombstone, I guess." His head rolled its eyes back into their sockets in mock exasperation, wobbled and floated back down behind its cubicle wall as the sound of typing commenced.

William smiled and asked, "Shouldn't that be 'grindstone?'"

"That's what I said, buddy." But Jensen's voice seemed to come from somewhere far beyond his cubicle, lower, as if he'd hastily crawled away, pressed his head against the floor and responded while his hands continued to type.

William glanced back to his welcome back card. Its thickness made it lay slightly open; at that angle, under the fluorescent lights' flicker, he thought he read an oddly cordial expletive in florid handwriting. But when he opened the card under direct light all the well-wishes become an amorphous mess again. He smelled the scorched coffee and his stomach clenched.

"Jensen, how do I get to the breakroom now? Looks like housekeeping made some changes." William waved in irritation towards the clutter of filing cabinets.

Jensen's arm popped up over the cubicle wall and gestured vaguely to his right. William heard him talking low, slurring into his phone. He walked towards the wall but didn't see the door's outline until he was standing just before it. The doorknob had been painted the same gray blue as the door and walls, the color of moldering fruit. The doorknob felt fuzzy, a slight brush of filaments tickled his palm. Once inside he swallowed three pills and chased them down with a large coffee cup full of water. The pressure in his chest deflated, the lights in his head dimmed.

William returned to his desk and performed his daily duties with perfunctory attention. The next eight hours rolled by with clockwork banality. Just twenty minutes shy of the end of the workday he realized his VP hadn't welcomed him back yet. It was the end of his second day back yet she hadn't called or even sent him an email. He found this strange, but chalked it up to the chaos of the company's financial difficulties and his own rather insignificant position in the corporate hierarchy.

He stood up to say good night to Jensen but he wasn't in his cubicle—in fact, he hadn't seen him since that morning. *Another day down, a lifetime to go*, William thought as he grabbed his coat to leave for the day.

Business Day 3

William's commute took him through older neighborhoods he didn't remember being so ominous. He couldn't recall details of the previous day's drive, but he *did* remember this part of the city hadn't always been so sparsely populated. The few folks he saw now were clearly homeless, but their rag draped figures stepped through the lopsided doors of ambiguous storefronts as if they owned the places.

He noticed the lack of law enforcement when he drove by a store whose entrance was a gaping hole surrounded by broken drywall and glass. He glimpsed furtive movements within, no doubt looters at work. On first try his cell phone wouldn't get any reception and when he finally received a few bars he dialed 911. But the call wouldn't connect and the ring continued in an odd drone. William chalked it up to atmospheric interference from the fog layer that coated the city and was all the talk on the news lately. The closer he got to work the denser the air became. The gritty fog shrouded the streets like a haze of spores clogging the city.

William didn't want to be here. He stared at the company's bright yellow logo prominently displayed on the entrance to the building. A bubble of anxiety grew inside him, expanded painfully against his brain. He took several deep breaths to calm the panic attack. He needed to get inside to wash down his pills with a glass of water or coffee. He clipped his dog-eared employee badge to his shirt pocket and walked for what felt like a lifetime to the entrance. He hesitated as the automatic doors failed to open, cupped his hands to the distorted glass to see if there was anyone inside.

A massive shape lurched towards the doors under the fluorescent lights inside. The ground shook violently. The door slid open in jolts, vibrating the floor, revealing the corpulent security guard pushing it aside. Stagnant air washed over William's face. He didn't recognize the guard. The fat man simply mumbled, "Power outage," and then walked back to his station, the back of his shirt umber from his copious sweat. He kicked up fat dust motes as he went. William removed his glasses and cleaned them with his shirtsleeve. When he replaced them the motes had diminished in size, yet the musty fog still permeated the air.

Jensen was bright and chipper first thing this morning. William couldn't see him but his enthusiastic voice projected far beyond his cubicle walls. "Morning, Will. Wanna see something?" He heard Jensen's question closer to his ears than seemed possible. His voice was phlegmy and padded, like he was speaking through the thickness of a furry growth. William looked over the cubicle's wall and Jensen was staring back, his wide smile flaunting tiny off-white teeth like the petite buds of mushrooms freshly burst through soil. "A break isn't gonna kill you. C'mon," Jensen insisted. William reluctantly agreed.

He followed Jensen down a side corridor he'd never been down before. The lights here were even dimmer than in his work area and the few that were on flickered and sputtered like gaslight. The air became progressively thicker and moister. They walked for about 10 minutes—William had never realized the building was so vast—then stopped at the entrance to a dimly lit, unpopulated room. Rows and rows of low-walled cubicles stretched out into the darkness.

Jensen turned to William, "Go on. Check it out."

"What? What do you mean?"

"The new department. The new VP's office is back there." William started to ask another question but Jensen shook his head impatiently and nudged him into the room. He walked slowly down the aisle, glancing at the empty cubicles on his left and right then back at a grinning Jensen. *You'll see*, Jensen mouthed silently. *Keep going.*

William walked deeper into the room until something enormous loomed above him, but it was just another barricade of filing cabinets topped off with chairs. As he continued around the barrier he noticed what appeared to be rusted metal buckets inside the cubicles. Every desk he passed had replaced their trash bin with shin-high corroded pails. He'd wandered deeper into the room than intended. He looked back toward Jensen but there was nothing silhouetted in the room's sole entrance. He detected a stronger stench underlying the mildew scented air.

"Hello? Jensen?"

Someone began typing on a keyboard somewhere deeper in the room. There was no glow visible from a monitor. William stared into the gloom and politely said, "Hi? Sorry if I'm interrupting."

The typing stopped. Several uncomfortable seconds passed. The unseen employee noisily cleared his or her throat. William started to explain himself while slowly walking back towards the exit's rectangle of light. The employee interrupted him with a hacking cough, each exhalation increasing in volume. William detected the clumsy squelch of something moving towards him. It sounded like mud stuffed burlap sacks lumbering down the aisle. The unmistakable odor of feces filled his nostrils.

William walked faster, not quite a run—there was no need to be rude to a co-worker, no reason to make their obvious handicap an issue. He should be more sensitive to other people's disabilities; they were probably walking with a prosthetic leg or a creaky old rolling walker. He didn't want to offend them but thought it best if he just quietly and quickly slipped out. He passed the mountain of filing cabinets and chairs, and then broke into a jog towards the exit. As he passed through the doorway into the less gloomy corridor something enormous crashed loudly behind him. Was that the stack of filing cabinets falling down? William broke into a sprint down the dank corridor, past several unoccupied offices back to his desk.

When William logged on to his computer to check his messages he saw that Jensen had been in a meeting for the last 45-minutes. He swallowed four more pills to calm his nerves and for a terrifying five-minute stretch forgot the name of his wife and daughter.

Business Day 4

The skies were gone. The city was inscrutable, the morning fog sloshed through the streets coating everything with a purplish gray film. William's morning commute took fifteen minutes longer than usual due to decreased visibility. It didn't matter much; he'd always arrived at work fifteen to twenty minutes early anyway. A migraine had infected his head, spreading to his jaw and neck. He'd already taken two pills this morning to calm the ache.

When he arrived at his desk he was surprised to see Jensen slumped in front of his computer so early—he usually sauntered in a good hour after William. If he were less tired and the pain in his skull less disorienting he would have seen that Jensen's torso wasn't collapsed like a rotting gourd, his head couldn't be a bulbous mass with indentations replacing his eyes. Jensen's mouth most certainly wasn't a grin stuffed with mold.

William logged onto his computer and was surprised to see an email from his VP. He stared at his monitor for several minutes, then distracted himself by straining to hear Jensen typing or sipping from his coffee mug. But the cubicle was silent. William knew he dare not look over the wall to say good morning. He opened the email. It was a one-on-one meeting invite for 8:30 a.m., just twenty minutes from now. Remembering that the new VP's office was a good ten-minute walk away, he grabbed a notebook and left his desk immediately.

The dank hall leading to the new VP's office had grown a thin layer of green-tinged fuzz. Or had it been repainted and William's migraine was confusing him? The air was definitely thicker and more humid than it had been yesterday. Spores were lazily floating about and William thought he saw a few that were as large as his eyeball, but his glasses must have been so dirty he was misinterpreting dirt on his lens. He entered the unlit room with its endless rows of abandoned cubicles.

The cubicle walls began to shudder slightly as if they'd anticipated William's arrival—definitely the result of his myokymia acting up again. The desk's surfaces seemed to glow with a pale luminescence that quivered under the air conditioning's flow but his growing migraine was the likely culprit for this optical illusion. William surprised himself by making good time; he had another seven minutes until the scheduled meeting.

He stopped to examine a cubicle more closely but the dim light prevented much clarification. He directed his cell phone's glow onto the corroded bucket he'd noticed the day before. It seemed to be bolted to the floor. As he glanced into the mouth of the bucket he saw that the bottom had been rusted out, exposing a hole that dropped down into the basement. He gagged and stumbled to one knee as the smell of sewage rose up from within. He tentatively tapped his heel against the bucket and was repulsed by the moist spongy texture. But his curiosity overcame his disgust and he lowered his cell phone's light closer to the object. It was a fleshy thing, an enormous mushroom with its cap inverted, the stalk's center hollow and dropping down into the pitch black cellar. He held his breath and peered into the hole, his phone held out like a flashlight. Within its depths, deep in the basement, a river of thick sludge glistened, a flow of what stank like an open cesspool.

William saw that what he had thought were bolts holding the pail to the floor were actually an outbreak of purple fungus spreading from the mass's base like malignant tumors. He stood abruptly as he realized the entire cubicle was undulating with thin hair-like rhizomes. They began to emit a ghostly glow, then faded into blackness again. He felt a wave of anxiety and horror rise in his chest as he accepted that he could no longer blame his migraine for what he was witnessing.

He knew none of this mattered anymore. He had long resigned himself to this career. He had wanted his wife and daughter to have something to remember him by, something they could actually look back on to substantiate that he wasn't a complete failure. But they were both gone before he'd done anything memorable. His wife had left a goodbye letter and in it she expounded on her philosophy of life and why she'd decided to take their daughter with her. She'd written that joy is to be found in varying degrees of misery; no intelligent person can ever truly be happy, they can only be less miserable than they were previously. William understood what she had meant. Life was decades of standing neck deep in sewage and happiness is attained when the filth retreats to waist level.

A baby started to cry from deep within the room. William immediately recognized his daughter's voice. He ran past a large unlit glass wall which had to be his VP's office. He ignored the massive glowing form that pushed against the other side of the glass wall and coughed his name repeatedly.

His daughter's voice rose in pitch and he knew for certain she was near. Her cries came from a cubicle to his left, within, inside one of the growths. He crouched over the open mushroom and caught a glimpse of something white drift by in the blackness underneath. He ran in the direction the flow took her.

William ran for hours. He was exhausted from the futility of running from the open mouth of one fungus to another, deeper and deeper into the endless aisles amongst the universe of cubicles. He examined hundreds, thousands of moldering and corroded cubicles, peering into the fungus's depths to find his daughter. He knew his strength would fade eventually. He knew he was inexorably lost amongst the infinite aisles. It was a hopeless task, searching an endless succession of empty cubicles for his daughter's face slipping by in the torrents of sewage under his feet.

After what must have been days of searching William stumbled into a cubicle and fell to his knees; his body could no longer match his determination. He hadn't heard his daughter's cries in hours, perhaps longer. He looked inside the fungus's throat and down in the basement's filth he saw his baby girl's face floating, milk-white in the black sick, honey-colored hair curls spread out. The dimensions of the mushroom's opening and his baby's head below were incongruous and distorted by a shift in his memory.

A gust of foulness rose from the depths. His girl's face, that oh-so-serious face like childhood rushing in a flood of emotion flowing into his head, his baby's face the most wonderful thing he'd ever remembered. The room seemed to melt into a tainted fog so all that was left was a void and a memory to fill the absence, memory like an island of debris in septic waters. He couldn't avert his gaze from his baby girl's eyes because the hole in the floor plunged deeper and the basement's sewage level rose as the fungus's fleshy rim stretched to envelop him. *I hate myself, I never should have been a father, I'm sweating from the oppressive heat of the office.* He struggled to gasp fresh air through the spore-choked air. He couldn't hear himself breathing anymore. His daughter was far too silent as the sewage gathered around her head and slowly closed over her pristine face.

NO ONE IS SLEEPING IN THIS WORLD

Architecture is the simplest means of articulating time and space, of modulating reality and engendering dreams.

-Ivan Chtcheglov, *Formulary for a New Urbanism*

I can no longer describe the droning songs as performed by the machines deep within the black bowels of the cities. I cannot accurately convey the process in which these gleaming threads bind me to the city's ribcage spandrels, their domes sprawled out like menisci on the surface of cosmic oceans.

An infinite array of cities swim through a sea of stars, megalopoli pass overhead adorned in streets and inhabitants and sputtering lights that inevitably blink into darkness. Klaxon horns scream with the enormous shriek of rusting metal, groan with the voice of split concrete. Ophanim wheels grind, propel existence into infinity.

My thoughts still drift to that day when the passage of time was still comprehensible. I remember the Alexei building pulling at our car like a maelstrom swallowing a boat. I remember clots of pedestrians wandering the sidewalk, aimless, heat damaged brains animating bodies like automatons. Even then they were alien to me, a multi-celled thing fidgeting on the surface of a Neubauer slide as I pretended my camera was a microscope.

I remember how it came to be that my soul was subsumed by architectural integration.

It was an unbearably hot summer day. Julia was driving. I saw something duck into an alley off of San Pedro Street. Of course it was just an emaciated dog with a disorder that made its skin appear wrinkled and shiny like a black plastic bag.

"We still shooting the haunted warehouse?" Julia sounded lethargic. The inflection in her voice made me yawn.

"It's not haunted. Ghosts are just how a city dreams about what it used to be."

"It's too fucking hot to get all metaphysical, sweetheart."

I laughed. "Of course we're goin'. Long as you got someone meeting us there, right?"

"Promised us the grand tour." Julia had stumbled across the Alexei building while collecting research material for our latest documentary *Landscape of Open Eyes*. A dream come true.

Alexei hadn't been a particularly prolific architect; he'd only crafted a handful of privately funded projects back in the mid 50s. His claims that his designs were drawn from dreams as well as his openly practicing a hodgepodge of occult ideologies branded him *enfant terrible* in the world of architecture. The stigma was understandable given his predilection for ignoring client's requests and adorning ambries with goat-headed cherubs or lunettes with ornate foliage and variations of Priapus, each progressively more lascivious. His mysterious disappearance in '68 and demolition of most of his works by the late 70s only exacerbated his reputation as a decadent architect and controversial artist.

I found it hard to believe there were undocumented examples of his craft tucked away in the heart of L.A., moldering into the compost heap of history. Every building he'd been associated with was tainted with a degenerate mystique, occupied by the ghosts of subversion and secrecy. This one had somehow escaped any scrutiny. Alexei's architecture was perfect fodder for *Landscape'*.

Filmmaking was Julia's calling, but architecture had always been my passion. In our college days the two of us would go on for hours about architecture and the theurgical expressions manifested in the world's structures. Initially we both romanticized what we were going to accomplish once we'd graduated and collaborated on various projects. We imbibed as many drugs we could afford on our limited budget, focusing on psychotropics which we saw as particularly effective in inducing altered states of awareness as a means to explore outsider art. We dabbled in mysticism, built increasingly convoluted Gysin machines, hallucinated while staring at prints of Karl Junker's murals in hopes his muse would touch us.

Our first film collaboration was *Thicket of New Veins*. In *Thicket'* we made the case that psychogeography had failed to enact any appreciable change in architecture. Footage of my vandalizing the Antilia building as a critique of wealth inequality and a nod to Chtcheglov's plot to destroy the Eiffel Tower got my visa to India revoked. Dissecting plastinated corpses to debunk Vitruvius' claim the human body was the epitome of architectural insight invited the grumblings of a criminal investigation. *Thicket'* had gained quite the cult following.

But our work in progress was different. In *Landscape'* we proposed that architecture was a brain template, cities neurons in the caudate. If one were to accept that sentience was predicated on matter, and cities were some of the most complicated structures ever built, emergent properties were the inevitable consequence. Aqueducts, avenues, sewers and axons; dendrite slopes, every street a glial cell. Infrastructure was just another ghost swarming with parasitic denizens, humanity a pack of animals dancing on the head of a flèche in the dreams of cities.

YHWH may have offered up redemption through Jesus, but the demiurgical whim that sparked all of creation did so through the architecture of the physical universe.

The car's a/c wasn't strong enough to combat the heat. Sleep pulled at me insistently. A klaxon's scream reverberated in my skull, damaged stereocilia made my eardrum throb. I'd suffered chronic ear problems since I was a child but the intensity of the pain was debilitating. I glanced out the car window. A massive face crept up an abandoned building half a block away.

When I removed my sunglasses the face became a heap of soiled cardboard boxes and battered shopping carts strewn from an open door onto the sidewalk.

But I recognized it from my dreams.

I often dreamt of alien lands, obelisks wrapped in parasitic vines, foliage leeching minerals from the stone; glass and resin buildings shaped into spirals of filigree; mile-high mounds of compacted soil, crumbling surfaces pocked with networks of tunnels. I'd catch furtive glimpses of unusual folk, presumably masked, peeking from strangely configured clerestory windows or behind columns sculpted from enormous vertebrae.

I never forgot those faces.

When I was a teenager I feared these dreams were a symptom of mental illness, but I eventually accepted the visions as the alchemy of my subconscious at play. Just another source of creativity.

I compiled volumes of notes in my secret book, covered the pages with poems and illustrations reminiscent of A.G. Rizzoli's art, though I could truthfully only give vague descriptions of my dream palaces. All too often I had to fall back on ambiguous observations like *cyclopean masonry vibrating*, the architecture *tasted like perfume*, or *hyperboloid ceilings with infinite expansion*.

The places I visited were overwhelmingly intricate and filled me with a kind of transcendental awe. As such my book was far more than a journal- it was a reminder of the various landscapes I'd explored and an attempt to capture a hint of what I'd experienced in those ineffable realms.

The car's monotonous whine colluded with the heat and my fatigue to keep snatching minutes away. I winced in pain. The klaxon horn's wail filled my head again. A thin shirtless man stood on the sidewalk urinating into a beer bottle. Julia maintained a stoic mask as she drove.

I thought we were in the Central Industrial area but I couldn't be sure. The street was dominated by rows of corrugated metal warehouses, the pavement strewn with burst trash bags and discarded clothing. A woman pounded her palm against the car as we drove by, her face contorted with rage. Everything felt wrong—I knew the homeless weren't feral animals squatting in waste, I was certain the city hadn't always been so tainted or misaligned. Exhaustion whipped up my anxiety.

We turned onto a block where the street signs were so encrusted with filth I couldn't read the names. "Any chance I could get some caffeine? I'm fadin' fast."

"Sure thing, princess." Julia muttered.

She parked next to the only convenience store we'd come across in the neighborhood. A few men across the street swapped cigarettes. I casually nodded at them. They didn't respond.

"Where are we?"

Julia shielded her eyes from the sun. "Skid row."

"Yeah, I know. But how close are we to the Alexei place? I've never seen this part of the city before."

"Not even in your dreams?"

Of course Julia meant it as a cynical joke about urban blight. I'd never mentioned my dreams to her before much less my dream book. I trusted her implicitly. Julia reminded me of who I used to be before the therapy and drugs and pressures from working on *Landscape'* dominated everything, before my life began to fade like chalk sidewalk art after thousands of feet had scuffed it away.

I checked my phone's map to see where we were but it loaded something that looked like a stain gasping for air. The street signs were covered in plastic trash bags duct taped to hold them in place. "You notice the signs?"

Julia stared down the block at something I couldn't see. She tapped her temple. "Sacred geometry Carla. Cities can mess with your head."

The sunlight left a grimy film on my skin. I realized I hadn't seen any traffic for awhile. Not even any parked vehicles.

"I'm goin' in. What you want?" Julia asked.

I told her. The store's windows were covered from top to bottom in yellowing posters advertising cigarettes and foreign beers in a script I didn't recognize. Several minutes passed. I debated following Julia inside to escape the sun.

A face floated down the street. A yellow clump in the sunlight, paper-thin expression kicked up by a slight wind that did nothing to alleviate the heat. The face fluttered closer.

I knew this thing, I'd seen it before. I wanted to run but felt ridiculous even contemplating the reality of any of this.

Two more floating heads joined the first, ochre colored and wrinkled as if mummified. *Que diablos esta pasando aqui?* A glob of sweat dripped from my eyebrow, stinging my left eye.

I laughed. The first face was just an old newspaper drifting aimlessly, its companion's grocery bags, expanding and deflating as a gust nudged them along.

When Julia returned with the drinks I didn't tell her what I'd seen. I was soaked in sweat, skin tight as if sun burnt. I guzzled the iced coffee. As we drove away Julia had to quickly swerve around a derelict poking around in the gutter. If she'd noticed his skin was wrinkled and bone white as a trash can liner she didn't mention it. I closed my eyes. Too fucking hot. Hallucinations from lack of sleep.

Julia drove a few more miles before pulling over near the curb. She popped a piece of nicotine gum into her mouth. "There she is in all her glory."

I was surprised to see that the Alexei building was just another corrugated metal warehouse surrounded by drab buildings, sheet metal peeling off in jagged layers. I paused, an overwhelming wave of nostalgia flowing through me as if I'd visited this place long ago. I took a few shots of the exterior as Julia gathered some film equipment.

"C'mon, look at it from this angle." I followed Julia to the corner of the warehouse.

From this vantage point I could see the tented roof and ornamental mascarons on the cornice like the faces of the dead crawling through the structure itself. I was reminded of buildings I'd seen in my dreams though this wasn't too unusual as Alexei's works were often milling around in my head. I took several more shots.

"Where's the guy we're supposed to meet?" I asked.

"About that…" Julia looked guilty.

"You're kidding me." I wasn't angry, Julia was notorious for little surprises like this.

"Property owner said the place is condemned or too dangerous or whatever for anyone to enter. Said if he let us in he'd be fined by the city or some bullshit." She waved her hand in the air as if fanning away the inconsequential details.

We already had plenty of footage for our film, mostly of the Bradbury Building and the L.A. Public Library with its mystical sphinxes and The Star of Ishtar, all under a pyramid roof topped with a serpent entwined hand bearing a torch—Luciferianism at its finest. But I was disappointed. This Alexei find would have expanded our work from the pedestrian to avant-garde.

"It's great and all from the outside but the inside has gotta be…." I trailed off.

"Agreed. We're screwed if we can't get the ok to film inside. But has that ever stopped us before?" Julia had a crazy grin on her face.

"Hell no."

"Then let's do this." Julia was a juvenile delinquent trapped in the body of a 28-year old artist. She hadn't changed much since we were kids.

We walked around the building. I was surprised to see there were no homeless people around. It was as if a city block radius around the place exuded a no-trespassing atmosphere.

"Found it!" Julia shouted.

She pointed out a rusty sliding shutter. Oddly enough it was the only surface free of any graffiti. There was no lock on the outside. Julia pulled on it but it wouldn't budge so the two of us grabbed the handle and worked together. Something snapped and it slid up.

The interior was even hotter and smelled like an abandoned abattoir, ripe with traces of slaughter. We stepped in and Julia pulled the shutter closed behind us. A grimy window allowed meager light to intrude. Julia's face was radiant in the dark.

"Ok lady. Ready for the grand tour?" Julia giggled in an uncharacteristically girlish manner.

I detected the faint sound of singing far off in the distance.

We checked the nearest doors but they were all locked. We explored a side hallway that ended abruptly, a pile of rusty equipment blocking the way. We backtracked and followed the main corridor which led us into a small dim room. A tall stack of wooden pallets lay rotting in the corner. Here the odor of dried offal was masked by a musky incense reminiscent of Mass. We stood before a massive metal sliding door that reached the ceiling high above. The handles were strapped by thick chains threaded through fist-sized holes plugged up with a leathery material.

I put my hand on the door and felt a faint vibration as if there was some kind of activity inside. When I placed my head up against the corroded metal it was too thick to hear anything distinct. I was crestfallen. The place seemed to be nothing more interesting than a dingy abandoned warehouse.

I cranked my camera's ISO as high as it could go and took some pictures but soon gave up. There was nothing here that attested to Alexei's touch.

"Nowhere else left to go." Julia said.

"What about up there." I pointed to a wide lintel that ran the length of the room and ended at an Oeil-de-boeuf window above the imposing doors. "If one of us can get up they'd be able to crawl to the window and see what's on the other side."

We set our camera equipment out of harm's way and dragged the decaying pallets closer to the wall near the window. In doing so we uncovered a large opening in the concrete behind them. A warm current pushed the sound of singing and the odor of greasy incense out of the gaping hole.

"You hear that?" I started filming in hopes of recording the sound. When I played it back there was nothing but white noise.

We moved the rest of the pallets and fully exposed the tunnel. It was a few feet wide and roughly waist high. A scattering of masonry powdered the floor. It looked like the passage connected to the room beyond the doors or at the very least ran next to it.

"I'm not turning back." I looked to Julia.

"Down the rabbit hole?" She flashed her tomboyish grin, her pupils as big as lens caps.

I turned my camera's flash on and took a few pictures of the tunnel to get a better idea of what was inside. We huddled around the image, the stark light exposing the crannies and fissures running through the concrete. I couldn't tell how far back the hole went. It extended into blackness.

We crawled on hands and knees side by side. There wasn't enough room for the film equipment so we each only carried a camera. About ten feet in the passage took a sharp right towards the room beyond the doors. I could see needles of dirty light poking through a grate not too far ahead.

The sing-song dirge grew louder.

We pressed up against the dead end, the gaps in the grate wide enough for us to see what was in the room. It was difficult to gauge just how large the area was for the shadows grew deeper the further the walls progressed and there weren't enough candles to illuminate the entire space. At least thirty people kneeled in the center, chanting something that sounded vaguely Gregorian if not for an undertone of gasping. I was shocked to see they all wore torn yellow raincoats and plastic trash bags over their heads like a parody of a mantilla.

"What the fuck?" I was immediately embarrassed; the whole display had a solemn pious air and I felt as if I'd just pissed in the baptismal font and dropped the baby. I was lucky that we were too far away for any of the worshipers to have seen or heard me.

Julia sounded giddy even while whispering. "You getting all this?" I gave a dismissive nod and continued to film the bag-heads. I tilted my camera to the ceiling where scant illumination filtered through the pigeon shit stained windows. I turned my camera to the architecture itself and gasped.

There were a few Alexei flourishes here and there but I thought the interior was more reminiscent of Piranesi's *Carceri* prints. Strange walkways that led nowhere swayed above, corroded cables and pulleys dangled from the darkness with unknown purpose- rusted metal staircases, rotting wooden ladders trailing off into nothingness. My heart pounded. I felt slightly drunk. The building stirred up something ominous inside me like silt disturbed at the bottom of a deep lake.

One of the bag-head's accessories of rags and fat plastic grocery bags seemed on the verge of bursting, transubstantiation in an L.A. warehouse. I recorded the woman then tapped my LCD screen in annoyance. The video played back a blurry 20-seconds of a sepia smudge, movement twitching in the center.

"Did the owner mention anything about renting the building out?" I spoke quietly but so emphatically it came out as a hiss.

"Sacred geometry Carla." Julia's teeth were bright in the gloom.

I knew we should've just left right then but there was a certain elegance in the sheer weirdness of the situation combined with the thrill of being part of an experience I'd never imagined—not even in one of my most outré performance pieces. Julia leaned in close to my infected ear and whispered *thank you*.

I was startled to see a rectangle of light appear on the cracked bricks of the warehouse wall. My gaze followed the dust mote filled cone of light back to a vintage Bell & Howell 16 mm movie projector tucked into a dark corner. The machine ran unattended.

Images of various civilizations flashed on the wall, forgotten cultures whose iconography and architecture seemed otherworldly like something from a Zdzisław Beksiński painting. Maps appeared, Haussmann's reconstruction of Paris, a clay tablet chipped with cuneiform. A bag-head stood up from the crowd with an open book in their hand. He began to read and I found it odd that the plastic over his face not only failed to muffle his voice his words actually resonated throughout the room:

Epidemiologists have known for decades that people who live in cities are twice as likely to become schizophrenic than those in rural areas. Neuroscientists have confirmed this hypothesis by demonstrating how the brain's structure is altered in city raised organisms.

The words were familiar but I couldn't quite place them. I was transfixed by the flickering images of the film though I had difficulty processing any sort of narrative content.

Not only has this biological change been conclusively shown, the evidence also suggests that the bigger the city the greater the risk for schizophrenia. The demiurge that constructed this architectural universe is intentionally altering the species to become conduits for dreams.

I saw myself projected against the wall.

I looked to be about 5-years old standing at the foot of my bed. The camera was shaky, my posture odd, limbs disproportionate compared to my torso. The film must have been edited with a clumsy jump cut for I suddenly materialized on top of the bed, my body violently convulsing. There was something wrong with the shape of my head, symmetries askew in suggestion of transmogrification. The camera jolted as if something had bumped it.

As Fulcanelli said: "The secret of alchemy is this: there is a way of manipulating matter and energy so as to produce what modern scientists call 'a field of force'. The field acts on the observer and puts him in a privileged position vis-à-vis the Universe. From this position he has access to the realities which are ordinarily hidden from us by time and space, matter and energy. This is what we call the Great Work."

Julia stared in astonishment at something on the stairs near the ceiling. Tears streamed down her beet red cheeks. The kneeling bag-heads all stood at the same time, rising like a dingy yellow cloud from a ruptured fungus. I looked above to see what everyone was looking at but there was nothing there.

I offer you the prisca sapientia of the Architect! I offer you the GREAT WORK!

Shadows in the corner of the room closed in. Black tendrils dripped from the ceiling, from the chaotic architecture, across the cement floor to the center of the warehouse where muscular strands danced in anticipation of great things.

I couldn't fathom what I was seeing. I tensed in anticipation of scrabbling back out of the tunnel but my world seemed to slow down while the building's internal geography hastened.

The inky appendages quickly congealed into a giant, its head a mass of billowing trash bags, each malformed bubble expanding and deflating repeatedly. Its arms were thick sheets of glass crudely cut into half moon shapes like scimitars, the surface stained and milky as slag glass. The head moved in such a manner it blotted out the space it occupied.

Time resumed. I began to crawl backwards but Julia pressed me up against the side of the tunnel. I couldn't move.

The monster vibrated with more intensity. Hairline fractures trickled across its glass arms. Its bulbous head wobbled like a liquid filled balloon caught in the runoff of a storm drain.

The bag-heads sang. Plastic sacks sucked into hollow mouths then exhaled boisterous hymns with the voice of klaxon horns. My ears leaked bloody pus. The warehouse reverberated with the screams of a billion decaying cities.

"Move, Julia!" Panic made my voice louder than I intended it to be.

"I'm sorry, Carla." She sounded sincerely apologetic, but continued filming whatever was going on in the main room.

"Julia?"

She grabbed my forearm with a fanatic's strength.

I was motivated by fear and adrenalin, consumed by an unthinking impulse to flee this situation. I elbowed my best friend with all my strength, felt something give. She rolled aside, both hands over her damaged face. I was crying with sorrow over hurting her and sobbing with rage that she had forced me to react this way.

I left Julia behind writhing in the narrow passage, her moans of pain following me. I backed out faster than I thought possible and finally exited into the small dark room.

I waited for her to come out. I wanted to beg forgiveness, shout at her for trying to keep us from escaping. Ask what was going on.

The rattle of the chains being undone on the other side of the huge door snapped me out of my reverie. The links slipped through the gaps onto the floor.

I ran down the dark hallway. Its curves and angles had mutated, its aberrant curvilinear design twisting and turning in such complex patterns I felt as if I'd covered miles before reaching the entrance. For one horrific moment the shutter refused to budge, and then it creaked and slid up. I stumbled onto the sidewalk, my eyes assaulted by the light.

The world was drenched in white.

The street was no longer asphalt and traffic signs but an expanse of wet gravel stretching off into a horizon the color of a blood clot. Rivulets trickled through the rocks where crosswalks used to be. The stifling atmosphere felt like a sheet of clear plastic had been stretched across the sky.

Baffled, I knelt down and brushed my hand across the ground. My palm was covered in chalky silt. The land was coated with several inches of the substance. There were tiny broken shells mixed in. The powdery marine sediment of tiny diatoms and the silica their skeletons left behind.

The city was dreaming of how it used to be.

I suddenly remembered where I'd seen the images in the film. They were my sketches. The bag-headed narrator had been reading from my dream journal.

I closed my eyes, resisted the lure of sleep. Even before I opened them I knew that the city's body had risen from the ground, domiciles ascending into a pink sky born of some mysterious chthonic activity. I was surrounded by mile-high edifices spun from glass glowing delicately in the diluted coral sunlight. The city's residents were active, peering at me with their unusual yet recognizable masks.

The bag-heads caught up with me. Their hands rough as concrete, nails sharp as broken glass. I retched as they dragged me back into the warehouse away from the alien landscape. The odor of stale blood overpowered the fresh scent of my wounds. I caught a glimpse of Julia in the crowd. She was wearing a filthy yellow raincoat. I knew that the next time I'd see her she would have already donned a trash bag face. The thought filled me with a tremendous loss.

They passed me down the long hallway into the heart of the Alexei church where that giant ragged shadow the color of waste clogging the drains leading to the sewers waited with outstretched gleaming arms. Its plastic bag gaze lingered like an old familiar face floating in all the world's gutters, in every entrance anyone had ever forgotten to close.

The city began to sing. My ears rang with the hymn of celestial horns and I lost the words to articulate what I'd once been and what I'd become.

MAKING SNAKES

Katryn was reluctant to talk to Alina about the powdery man. It had happened so long ago, and she wasn't sure she could trust her sister anymore; her face had started to move around on the skull and her mouth no longer matched her words.

"There was nobody there." Katryn stood in the open doorway, hands clasped together. She spoke softly, as if afraid the unseen visitor might still be within earshot.

"I don't know how the reporters keep getting past the gate." Alina said.

"But there wasn't anyone at the door." Katryn was certain the powdery man had returned, but she wouldn't burden her sister with her suspicions. She loathed her body. Repulsed by her thoughts. Her own voice disgusted her.

Alina sighed with a heady mix of sympathy and frustration. "I'm sorry sis', but the press can be far too aggressive. We all truly want to help you move on."

"My fault." Katryn's words felt childish and petulant in her mouth.

"Oh dear. I don't like it when you're in *this* mood." Alina sipped her coffee. Steam coated her glasses. Eyes transformed into orbs of fog. "You have to return that terrible agent's phone calls soon. What is his name? No matter. You need to speak with him."

Katryn excused herself to the comfort of her bedroom. She slid her fingertips across the spines of her favorite books in contemplation of which to read again. But she knew she'd never get around to it. None of this mattered. Her vocation had ended just as quickly as it had ascended. She was now nothing more than grist for the Hollywood rags, a whipping post for the savage gossip of the Hedda Hoppers and Louella Parsons.

Contemplating the irrelevance of resuming her acting career lessened the pain, eased her despair somewhat. She'd never entertained the notion anything was waiting beyond the veil; all she had to look forward to was the very same eternal abyss that loomed before conception.

What did one more film project or theater role matter? Antitrust rulings and the overwhelming influence of the National Legion of Decency had hindered here career opportunities. It mattered little; art was a conceit, another distraction from the banality of living. Everything ultimately ended.

Later that evening, long after Alina had locked all the doors and retired to her own room, Katryn saw movement beneath her door. She pressed her cheek against the floor and watched the fleeting shadows of bare feet running past her room.

Girlish voices whispered in the hallway, faded as they ran out the kitchen door into the woods, crashed through the foliage. They injured their soles on the forest floor and their cries floated above the nocturnal clicks and hums of insects.

Katryn was just a child when she first encountered the powdery man. She'd been playing in the abandoned lot, a dumping site where all kinds of interesting trash was strewn about in the yellow thigh-high grass, brittle and itchy.

A jalopy had pulled up, parked on the outskirts of the field. She distinctly remembered the truck's presence disturbing the grass, a spreading ripple in a peculiarly textured wave, stalks shaking like broom bristles. The driver had shouted something but Katryn hadn't been able to make it out. She'd walked closer to the vehicle.

The man's eyes were deeply set in a wrinkly face powdered with stage makeup, like an actor from the silent era. A cigar dangled between his gray lips. He spoke in the high pitched voice of a prepubescent boy.

Wanna make snakes?

Katryn hadn't known what the powdery man meant by this, much less why it terrified her.

She screamed.

He'd tossed his cigar into the dry grass, stepped out of his truck, gestured for her to approach. His eyes and skin had fouled the air with something more threatening than physical harm, a portent of apocalyptic dread that lingered in Katryn's memory to this day. He'd removed his tweed cap. His bald head had been white with powder.

His hands stretched impossibly long, fingertips flowing into keratin tipped darts. He'd moved towards her with an awkward gait, stiff, as if learning to walk with prosthetic legs.

Katryn ran from the lot. She didn't stop until she'd reached her front porch and any further details of the experience were lost in a fog of distant memories.

"I think our house is haunted." Alina raised an eyebrow conspiratorially. She stirred her black coffee until the liquid spiraled on its own. "Isn't that delightful?"

Alina's hair was a miasma of black fog jiggling around a puffy sleep deprived face. Katryn hoped this was due to the indigo window casting a shadow above. She couldn't be sure; there was more stained glass in her childhood home than she remembered and the walls and floors were painted in floral hues that changed their brightness and shade inconsistently.

"I've heard nothing." Katryn was grateful for her sister taking her in when she needed help, but she was ashamed at how easy it had become to lie to her. Her hands felt swollen. She moved the larger of them away from her cup. Hid the offending extremity beneath the table top.

"You believe in spirits?" Alina asked.

"No. Nothing more than this." Katryn rapped the table with her fingers. "All we can do is make believe the spurts in our heads are more meaningful than pebbles smoothed by a stream."

"I don't understand. You never make sense, sis'. I thought you artists were all mystics and poets." Alina gave a reassuring smile. "Ghosts and luck and 'break a leg' and all that."

Katryn thought about the girls running between the trees, over brambles and jagged branches. They might be lost. Maybe they were being chased by the powdery man.

There must be someone who cared about them, worried about their well being. She suddenly realized she'd been about her daughter's age when she'd last played in the field.

She'd scampered up the back yard's cherry tree (these days it was barren and withered like the backdrop for some gothic stage production), dropped down on the other side of the fence. Traced her familiar path to the empty lot. She hadn't been concerned about the powdery man showing up then; she'd kept to the edges of the field close to her well worn trail home. This was her secret playground. She hadn't even considered relinquishing it to anyone.

Kicking at corroded pipes and pieces of broken furniture had been sufficient entertainment until she came across a stained toilet tilted on its side. She'd peeked inside the bowl.

A little girl's head stared back at her.

Skin greasy like crinkled wax paper. Hair lopsided as if wearing a filthy wig that hadn't fallen all the way off. Insect activity convinced Katryn it wasn't a mannequin.

The corpse's eyes were wide open. Opaque. Beautiful opalescent pearls.

This world, Katryn thought, *this ugly world*. At that moment, at that tender age, she knew that everything was destined to end up waste abandoned in places nobody visited anymore.

Something subtle changed in the air. An engine roared. She knew it was the powdery man's antique vehicle. She'd sprinted away as fast as she could.

"Penny for your thoughts?" Alina gently touched her sister's arm. Her voice brought Katryn back to the room, back to her large hand touching the smooth warm surface of her cup.

Katryn shook her head.

Alina rubbed her neck in exasperation. "Please. I'm here for you. I really am. But please," she said in a tone Katryn had never heard her use before.

"I'm sorry."

"We just want you to get back to work on the set. The production needs you. You can't keep blaming yourself. Little girls and accidents, well..."

"Everything's an accident." Katryn finished her coffee then returned to her room. The faucet dripped onto the broken ceramic basin in the bathroom. Her sister had removed the barbiturate bottles and taped up the cracked sink to prevent any further injuries on the sharp edges.

Katryn had always known that the powdery man waited for her.

Vibrating between the wrinkles in this world.

Waiting for her to become a parent, to become successful on the stage and screen.

Waiting for her to reach her darkest hour before making his grand appearance. For the drugs to make her so weary she could no longer fend him off.

The last time she'd seen him was in her old home in the Pacific Palisades. Hovering in the corner of her bedroom, his cigar's cherry the only splash of color in that dismal space. Wet lips opening and closing like the tearing of a birth caul.

Wanna make snakes?

This was all he'd say.

Repeatedly.

Fingers wriggled like snakes. Elongated into darts that stretched through the dark to caress Katryn's skin. Her sheets had retained the warmth and shape of her daughter who'd swallowed far too many pills and was sleeping far too peacefully and all Alina had been able to say was *I am so sorry* far too many times to be of any consequence.

Katryn spent the early evening reading scripts in her room. A flash of white outside the window caught her attention.

The girls ran across the yard.

They wore flimsy tattered garments. Hair scraggly and wild. They were all barefoot. The flesh on their damaged feet trailed behind like ribbons, shining wetly in the waning light.

Katryn walked quickly yet quietly through the house past her sister's bedroom. Alina was breathing in a ragged rhythm. She slipped out the front door and gently closed it behind her.

She ran after the girls.

They raced through the woods, mutilated feet further torn by thorns and sharp stones. Ran over open dusty fields and barren landscapes. Passed through back yards, the houses' windows glowing with odd light.

They circled back to Katryn's childhood secret field. The land was surrounded by a rusty fence. Several sections had been stomped down by those who'd continued to dump trash. The girls slipped across the field like wisps of fabric in the wind.

The sky was red. The air filled with cicadas singing a dry song. Katryn couldn't explain how she knew, but she was certain there were hundreds of little girl's decomposing heads buried in the landfill.

Her eyes watered at the intensity of the late sky. The garbage and the decay of this place filled her vision. The lot looked as false as a plywood backdrop propped up by fragile two-by-fours.

The insects ceased their noise. Nothing moved save for the subtle shuddering of the long, stringy weeds growing from beneath the flat tires of a long abandoned derelict truck.

The buried heads began to whisper to each other.

Pale flakes of makeup fell from Alina's face. Someone had failed to light the room properly; her lips were an unhealthy color. The shade of a sickly flame behind a gray glass candle sleeve.

"The doctors have gone over this again and again. You weren't yourself." Alina touched Katryn's hand, her skin gritty as if covered in powder. "You need to go back before the end of the week or the producers are going to find someone else."

The morning chill seeped from the wooden floor through Katryn's bandages into her damaged feet. The sensation was pleasant.

"She knew they weren't candies." Katryn gave a weak smile. She looked out the window at the tops of lush trees rippling like the surface of an ocean in the wind. "I'm responsible. If not for me—"

Someone knocked at the front door.

"Oh dear. Do you hear that? They're nosing about again." Alina stood, walked towards the entrance.

Katryn stared out the window and watched the girls run between the trees. Their diaphanous rags glowed in the lambent light. Several had fingernail thin darts protruding from their shoulder blades and calves.

The foliage shuddered as something unseen chased them.

A bump against the front door. The window panes clinked in response. "Hold on. No need to be rude."

The door shook violently.

"You hear that dear? Such impatience."

"I don't know what I heard," Katryn said.

Alina opened the door.

THE OCEAN IS EATING OUR GRAVES

Levi and Mariee were seven years old when they found the dead child on the shore. The newborn's skull was horribly deformed: bulbous eyes, skin the color of a Moon Jellyfish, a face so unlike the twins they were certain it wasn't human. Despite Levi's attempts to console Mariee, she wept as if they'd lost a sibling.

The Coastal Colony Tribes' reservation police investigated, but nothing was resolved. It was several years before AIM and the Ogala Lakota took over Wounded Knee, so few non-Indians were aware of, much less cared, about Native human rights issues. Predictably, outside authorities claimed the corpse's deformities were the inevitable consequence of Indians and alcohol.

But that malformed baby stirred up talk on the Rez. Stories about *Pugwis* and *Kushtakas* luring children to a watery grave spread, and a few influenced by *Kwakwaka'wakw* myths spoke of *Kumugwe* lurking just off the coastline.

Levi's tsunami nightmares started the evening the elders buried the tiny corpse.

When Levi was a child he'd pretend the windswept Douglas Firs leaning away from the ocean were Tsimshian totem poles trying to escape the icy spray. The pieces of glass-smooth driftwood washed up by foamy waves were magical artifacts. It was a landscape plucked from another world and spliced with the local fauna in hopes the invasive species would eventually replace his land.

"Well, look what the sea washed up." The deep voice startled Levi.

Dr. Alex Hardy still sported long, braided hair and turquoise bracelets. Still playing the Indian wannabe. Levi didn't remember his old professor's eyes being such a vivid blue.

"Good to see you. Hope you don't mind that I used some vacation time to poke around." Levi said.

"Glad you could visit off the clock, Dr. Garcia. Let me show you what we've found."

Levi did his best to hide his annoyance over Applied Environmental, Inc. hiring Dr. Hardy to work on Site 35-CS-198. Granted, the Coastal Colony Tribes Rez relied on contractors since their cultural resource budget was limited, but he felt stifled bound to a desk at the State Historic Preservation office. He missed the archeological work, the saturated ground under his boots, the subtle tug and depth of ancient things buried within the land. The world of fossil antlers and osteological jungles deep below seemed far too distant as of late.

The Blood Mound was monstrous, several feet taller than Levi's impressive height. The clay was a deep, reddish chocolate color, like a swollen blood blister. The crew had sectioned the dome into balks, partitions breaking it up into four quadrants to better preserve its stratification. There were several archeologists and students digging and sifting in the deep wet sand.

Levi placed his palm on the mound. The clay suckled his flesh. He rubbed thumb against forefinger, fascinated and repulsed by the soil's color and albumen-like texture.

"Hiker found a bone fishhook over here. Our initial survey uncovered the top of the clay and we've since excavated the whole thing."

Levi resisted the urge to scour the red stain from his skin. "Any idea what it's for?"

"Not a funerary receptacle. Plenty of lithic and bone tools inside—harpoon points and such. No human remains. We've catalogued and stored the artifacts in town at the rental space. Waiting to be shipped off to the university lab."

"Most of these kinds of mounds were used for burial. Nothing like the Etowah or Gahagan mounds."

"No. Nothing like them."

"Clay?"

"The Structural Geology lab is going over the samples. I'll e-mail you what they've sent so far."

Levi wasn't surprised that little had changed on the Rez—same tilt of a rusted fence, same growth of mold enveloping a crumbling home, rows of abandoned houses, roofs sagging with age. All casualties of bank-redlining the American Indian Housing Council was powerless against. He imagined everyone lying in their soggy beds and couches as they grew into the furniture like moss on roof shingles.

He drove to the outskirts of the reservation into the small town of Mosswood, past the convenience store's alley where Thomas had suffered irreparable brain damage from huffing paint thinner, past the trailer park where the Reynolds brothers beat 15-year-old Levi so severely he missed a week of school. He'd made sure the Reynolds boys missed a month.

He parked at the River Run Café. As he set foot on the asphalt something scurried past his truck. Probably a stuffed trash bag swept along by the rushing waters. His rain-saturated glasses only made the object look like a blubbery animal waddling through the muddy ditch.

Mariee was waiting for him inside, the café's only customer. She was wearing their old high school punk band sweatshirt, *Red Menace.*

"Oh, sweetheart, your hair used to be as black as the ocean floor."

"Hey, go easy, sis—I'm here on vacation."

"What's it been? Ten months?"

"Nine months. Congrats on your promotion, by the way."

"Thanks. I'll let you get away with changing the subject."

Her smile was infectious. Mariee had always been better at learning languages and absorbing foreign cultures than Levi—there was no one better qualified for the Tribal Historic Preservation Officer role. He was proud of his twin sister.

Mariee slid a key towards him. "I don't care if your room is on the state's dime; my place is closer to the site than any shitbox hotel in Mosswood."

"Thanks. You're pretty considerate for a Rezzy 'crat."

"I am, aren't I."

Levi tried to enjoy his grilled salmon and eggs breakfast, despite the strange consistency of the fish. Several cups of coffee and a basket of warm fry bread washed the disconcerting aftertaste away.

"How'd your visit with Dr. Hardy go?"

"He's a bit different than I remember. So, is this where you tell me why you think he violated NAGPRA?"

Mariee's suspicions relied on the word of Adam Joseph, a Duwamish kid recruited to the site on an SAA Native American Scholarship. Adam claimed he'd been sorting fish bones at a flotation tank when he saw Dr. Hardy walk off with a parietal bone.

Levi traced his finger along the FUCK THE REZ groove carved into the tabletop. "Stealing Indian bones, federal shitstorm like that—" he paused with a mouthful of bread, "—needs more than the word of some student."

Mariee nodded. "I don't want to ruin anyone's career, but Adam also found a strange artifact. Photographs it, fills out an area form, bags and labels it. Archeology 101. Adam checks the database the next morning and ...."

"Never entered."

"You got it."

"You really think Hardy is a goddamn pothunter?"

"Maybe. Adam texted some pics." Mariee handed her phone to Levi.

There were several shots of a cylinder, bone or ivory, stained a dull red from the clay it had been buried in. The surface was etched with unusual designs that didn't resemble any Native art Levi was familiar with.

"Haven't heard or been able to get a hold of Adam since he sent these last Tuesday." Mariee's voice quavered.

"Probably ran off with a girl." Levi knew he wasn't offering much comfort. Violent crime on the Rez had escalated dramatically and they both knew how the machine operated—justice was all-too-often stymied by convoluted federal jurisdictions. Another disease inherited from the European occupation as far as Levi was concerned. He deftly changed the subject.

"Hardy might be a respected anthropologist, but to me, he'll always be just another academic appropriating Native cultures. Remember back in college? Arrowhead necklaces and all that turquoise jewelry. Fucking joke."

"Sometimes, we have work with whatever's available. Enemy of my enemy and all that." Mariee sounded uncharacteristically angry.

Levi shrugged. "Christ, those lectures on telepathic dolphins and Von Daniken pseudoarcheology ...." He mimicked Hardy's baritone voice: "Lacandon Mayans are from Mars; Tz'utujil are from Venus."

Mariee couldn't help but laugh. "Crazy shit, innit? Almost as crazy as that Blood Mound."

That night, Mariee went to bed early while Levi stayed up to read the lab reports Hardy had e-mailed. Salmon, duck and deer bones dating back to the late 17th century, plenty of faunal material, traces of camas bulbs mixed into the oak and pine charcoal samples. There was little doubt in his mind that 35-CS-198 was a temporary settlement swept away by the Cascadia tsunami.

In 1700, a massive earthquake had caused a tidal wave to sweep from Vancouver Island to Northern California, sinking the Washington coastline by as much as 3.5 meters. Geologists estimated that the area's subduction zone produced a massive tremor every 500 years on average—the region was long overdue for another one. Levi was certain his tsunami nightmares would be brutal that night.

He skimmed the geology lab's results: *Deposition of fine-grained sediments on the continental shelf... Abyssal deposition of clays... found in submarine canyons...* The Blood Mound contained volcanic ash, silica shells, hematite. That explained the red color.

The rubidium-strontium tests identified the clay samples as pelagite, a sediment found far from major landmasses. At depths below 6,000 meters.

The lab must have made a mistake.

There were a couple of species on the spreadsheets he hadn't expected to see—an abundance of *Chauliodus macouni* and *Abyssobrotula galatheae* bones, more commonly known as the viperfish and cusk eel. Both animals inhabited the Abyssal and Hadal zones, in the furthest trenches of the oceans. Well over 10,000 meters deep.

Almost seven miles underwater.

Levi was sure this would all make more sense after a good night's rest.

He dreamt he was writhing in bloody clay, devouring nutrients in the stagnant muck, gorging on decomposing bones, ferns and rotting larvae. The clay filled his eyes and mouth. A tsunami rose miles into the sky, descended and rolled across the cosmos. Something began to sing. When he woke up he assumed Mariee had walked to work since her bed was made and her car was still in front. As he sipped his coffee his ears rang with the dream song.

Levi decided to avoid 35-CS-198 for the day and catch up on old acquaintances. As the afternoon approached, he called Mariee to see if she wanted to join him in Mosswood for lunch, but her voice mail picked up.

By early evening he tried Mariee's cell and work numbers again with no luck. This was unlike her; she was obsessively punctual. Her Umpqua women's advocacy group had probably run later than expected. He thumbed through the literature on her bookshelves in hopes he'd see something that would draw his attention away from the phone.

Mariee had always been an avid reader, mainly history and sociology. But her bookshelves also held yellowing fantasy novels whose plots centered on barbarians battling tribes that were thinly veiled racist stereotypes and sci-fi covers depicting bipedal *axolotls* rising from the depths to rape the surface world's women. Literature that warned against the threat of miscegenation.

But Levi knew that Mariee saw something beyond his knee-jerk assessment. To her, they were not only thrilling adventures but a way to explore fantastic lands guided solely by imagination. Perhaps, in some subtle way, these books had inspired her to study their own Coos heritage, free of Eurocentric impositions.

One particular book's spine caught Levi's eye. It was a limited print vanity press edition titled *Unidentified Aquatic Objects* by an I.T. Ivan. The blurb read, "Ever Wonder Why 89% of UFO Sightings Are Near Water?" then elaborated by alleging UFOs (or UAOs) were emissaries from underwater alien bases.

Levi thought back to college and remembered Hardy's office stacked with books on Lemuria, Pumapunku, and "ancient astronaut" titles. For some inexplicable reason, he distinctly remembered a copy of *Unidentified Aquatic Objects* on the desk.

He was acting paranoid. Mariee just happened to have the same obscure volume Hardy had all those years ago. But the coincidence, combined with the missing Duwamish kid, the artifact and human bone, clawed at his gut. Hardy had stored his finds at the Mosswood storage facility. The building *was* isolated. The area *was* a convenient spot to hide something…

Levi threw the book back on the shelf. He was being ridiculous. Dr. Alex Hardy was a renowned archeologist, not a thief, much less a psychopath. He had to think this through rationally. But he also knew he was wasting time, pacing his sister's house waiting for a phone call.

Levi parked his truck in front of Mosswood's sole storage facility. The sliding shutters for the individual rental spaces were labeled, but he looked for the only one with a padlock. He quickly found it.

Getting caught would have serious repercussions, but he was betting his crime would be blamed on bored teen vandals. He kicked the shutter several times until the metal loop holding the lock in place broke away.

Inside, rows of corrugated plastic Hollinger boxes were stacked on wire shelves running the length of the small room. They were all marked with a CV-7421 sticker identifying their contents as originating from the Blood Mound site. Levi opened a few to find labeled polyethylene bags stuffed with animal bone chips and mussel shells.

Sweat trickled down his temples. He pointed his flashlight inside another box, all the while dreading the discovery of human bones. He glanced over his shoulder at the broken door, expecting something to come bursting in. There were only painted shells and dozens of faded beads that had been brightly colored centuries ago.

Nothing incriminating. He'd let his personal dislike of Hardy lead him on a wild goose chase—not to mention breaking and entering. He'd allowed his impulsiveness to get the better of him.

His phone vibrated. He was disappointed to see it was Hardy's number.

"Alex?" He felt as if he'd been caught red-handed, but managed to keep his voice steady.

"We need to talk." Hardy's voice gurgled unpleasantly.

"About Mariee?"

There was a long pause. "They've gone and summoned it. It's

ascending—"

"Meet me at the River Run Café." Levi interrupted.

He slid into the booth across from Dr. Hardy. The waitress came by and Levi ordered two coffees.

Hardy was pale, his skin oily, almost sleek in the diner's diffused light. "It can't walk and it can't multiply, so let it be merely a thought."

"The Popol Vuh." Levi shook his head in confusion. "What is this about?"

"At first, the gods made them from clay, but the water dissolved their bodies. Like Cairns-Smith's clay from silicates, crystal structures proliferating, each layer containing defects allowing natural selection to influence their growth."

Levi couldn't disguise his frustration. "Is there a point to all of this?"

"The Koran says humans came from a clot of blood. The Sioux have *We-Ota-Wichash*, Much Blood Boy, the—."

"I know. Some of us were born real Indians. But I'm not sure why you think I give a fuck about Sioux legends—we Redskins don't all have the same customs. Where's Mariee?"

Hardy looked hurt. "Mariee called them *Pugwis*. I thought, if I ever published a paper on them, I'd call them *Abyssal Ones*—" He laughed and made a dismissive gesture.

"Your students might be impressed by your alien fantasies, but I'm not. Where's Mariee?"

The waitress brought their coffee. Hardy spoke when she was out of earshot. "A new people, Levi, an undiscovered culture."

Levi wasn't ready to accept submersible ETs burying their kin in native burial mounds. "Alex. Did you steal artifacts? Take some bones as souvenirs?"

"Oh, their technologies..." Hardy looked as if he were going to weep. "They can do things with biology we've never even come close to imagining."

"What did you do to my sister?"

Hardy looked at his work-weathered hands on the table. "She dove deeper than any human has ever been."

It took everything in Levi to keep from reaching across the table and hurting the elderly archeologist, but he managed to calmly drop a five on the table and walk away. None of this mattered anymore; all he'd gained from the conversation was that the senile old fool was still obsessed with space devils and indigenous tall tales.

It all seemed futile. Mariee had only been gone a day, at most, and he knew that, what with the rise in violent crime, the Rez police would be too busy to halt everything for an overprotective brother. He drove back to his sister's place.

As he walked to the front door he heard something move through the grass at the back of the house. Probably a raccoon raiding a trash can.

The living room was dark and quiet. The kitchen pet door Mariee had refused to tape shut after her cat disappeared a week ago made a loud swooshing noise.

The linoleum floor glistened with what looked like frog eggs. The ooze led to the cat flap. Levi cleaned up then lit scented candles to remove the stench of decomposing fish.

Something caught his attention through the kitchen window. The door to the tool shed was open, the entrance blacker than its surroundings.

He walked across the small backyard. The trash cans hadn't been disturbed. He turned the shed's single light on. The interior was cluttered with Hollinger boxes, all labeled CV-7421.

"Not you, sis." His voice sounded strange in the enclosed space.

The boxes held bags stuffed with human vertebrae, teeth, a fragment of a tibia. A partially intact skull wrapped in acid-free tissue paper.

The bones were sanguine from the clay they'd rested in for centuries. Several were drilled with tiny holes—Levi thought it likely anemia damage, but the cavities were unusually small and there were too many of the pockmarks for him to make a definitive diagnosis. He pulled out another box. A subtle shift of weight made it clear there was something larger within than individual bones.

Inside, its head wrapped in Ethafoam packing, was what he initially mistook for a small *Hylobatidae*. On further examination he realized it was human, despite the length of the ulna and radius and the four grotesquely long phalanges on each hand. The creature had seven true ribs but too many false and floating ones—more like bristles, a thin comb attached along its thoracic vertebrae. The metatarsals were elongated and bent at the wrong angle.

Its anatomy was unlike anything he'd ever held or seen in any journal. He removed the protective wrapping around the head.

The skull's smooth inion suggested she was female. Someone had painted symbols all over her cranium in the same script with which the missing bone cylinder relic had been etched.

The face was a horror. Jaws rooted with pin-like teeth, enormous orbital cavities—*all the better to absorb what little light was available at the bottom of the sea,* Levi thought. For a moment, he nearly convinced himself it was a Jenny Haniver someone had made as a hoax.

Maybe she'd been ravaged by mutations, afflicted with a disorder that just happened to twist the body into something that resembled an organism accustomed to life in the ocean's depths. Or maybe he was looking at some newly discovered body modification like those once practiced by the Chinook, something that altered their shape far more than cradle boarding could ever achieve.

But he was well aware that none of these adaptations came from cradle boarding or binding. He thought of ancient things his ancestors believed skulked at the outskirts of society, tentatively treading closer to civilization.

It was all a lie. Mariee accusing Hardy, luring him to the reservation-even the specifics of Adam's involvement were likely fabricated.

There was only one other place Mariee might be.

He drove towards the coast as fast as he could navigate the rain-slick roads. He left his keys in the ignition and clambered down the path to the beach. The clay mound was an ominous silhouette against the sand and sky.

A large section of the Blood Mound had been leveled into a makeshift shrine, the ledge lined with driftwood sculptures of various sea creatures that appeared to be either poor interpretations of known species or animals whittled from imagination. The display surrounded the skeletal remains of something infant-sized. Its head was buried in a pile of seashells.

Levi yelled for Mariee once, then again. When there wasn't any

Christopher Slatsky

response, he went to examine the altar up close.

The skeleton had a similar morphology as the creature in Mariee's shed. Its phalanges were intact save for a missing distal on the right hand. Its remaining fingers were still curled around the stolen bone artifact. He gently moved its hands aside and picked up the cylinder. Its weight and texture confirmed it was ivory, probably whale. The writing was still incomprehensible, but Levi could make out details such as strange starfish things with too many appendages and vaguely familiar sea animals, their faces inexplicably anthropomorphized.

The indentations reminded him of Braille. Something shifted in his brain and he suddenly knew this scrimshaw was a series of prayers that could be read in a realm where light couldn't penetrate. Nausea swirled in his stomach when he thought about what exactly this shrine was meant to appease.

Levi carefully placed the creature's hands back over the artifact then brushed aside the accumulation of shells hiding the head. The skull was even more disfigured than the specimen in the shed, but also decorated with the same pictograms and script.

He stared past the Blood Mound to the sea. Shadows flitted beneath the waves.

For a few moments, he thought it was a school of sardines thrashing around in the waters. When a phosphorescent glow began to spread he knew something else was responsible. Levi backed away from mound.

Something burst from the water.

His mind couldn't quite interpret what he was seeing. The vague notion that an albino ribbon worm rose before him into the air so high it might punch through the clouds was all he could process. Its tubular body glowed with an inner luminescence, radiant against the black rain clouds as it swayed in place. The stench of organic matter long decomposing on the ocean floor wafted across the beach.

Levi inadvertently whispered, *Kumugwe*.

But this *Kumugwe* was not the majestic undersea god draped in copper finery the elders had told Levi and Mariee about when they were children. This god bore the striations and scars of age. Necrotic matter dangled from it in tatters as if shedding old skin to birth something new. Its hide was so white Levi could see arteries pushing fluids beneath.

Dozens of *siamang*-sized *Pugwis* the color of clam meat scurried across *Kumugwe*.

The worm roared. Its head split into several triangle- shaped sections, each flap billowing like wind-filled sails. Something squirmed in what Levi surmised was its mouth. Water fountained from the opening into the night sky.

Not water but a mass of thin, translucent cords whipping the air.

The beach swarmed with *Pugwis*. A groping, clumsy mob, their limbs not yet accustomed to an atmosphere free of water resistance, bulging eyes not yet adapted to this new, brightly lit world.

A creature brushed against Levi, its flesh the texture of a jellyfish. He couldn't help but be astounded that he'd actually touched an organism unknown to science. *Kumugwe* lowered its head, with Levi in the direct path of its vast maw.

Ropy strands vomited from the mouth. Levi pushed one of the *Pugwis* into the filament's path. The strands impacted the flabby horror with such force it was sent careening like a paper doll caught in gale force winds. When the hair-thin filaments squirmed over its bare skin, sank into its flesh and dragged the flailing body towards the sea, Levi understood why the bones in the shed had been riddled with so many tiny holes.

Several *Pugwis* sensed their kin's blood. They swarmed over it in an orgy of decadent hunger as the doomed victim slid across the sand towards *Kumugwe*'s gaping mouth.

Levi ran past the Blood Mound.

The *Pugwis* seemed more interested in exploring than pursuing Levi. He reached the top of the hill and crouched behind some foliage, his view to where the ocean lapped at the edge of the Blood Mound unobstructed. There were now hundreds of the things frolicking up and down the beach and over the clay mound. He could make out the details of their long-fingered hands, digits connected by a layer of flesh, mouths dangling open far too wide, filled with crooked teeth jutting out at odd angles.

A *Pugwi* stopped its examination of the mound and stared up the hill. Levi was afraid to move for fear of revealing himself, just in case the creature hadn't yet pinpointed his hiding spot. The thing's gaze filled his head like unblinking black stars. An alien mind caressed his mind.

It revealed its history to him. They'd been trying to make contact shortly after he and Mariee had discovered one of their hybrid dead. His sister understood them better than he ever could—where he'd seen nothing but tsunami nightmares, Mariee had glimpsed their history and faith, their needs and desires. The twins had been ambassadors between the aquatic world and humanity, but Mariee had been the only one aware of that role.

Levi sprinted to the truck.

As he sped away he risked glancing back at the ocean. *Kumugwe* quivered in the air, darkness spreading beneath as if the worm were bleeding shadow.

Something incomprehensibly large was ascending.

Levi knew then that this was not *Kumugwe* in its entirety. This massive entity was a single tentacle, a fragment, a strand of a swimmer's hair floating on the surface as the bulk of its form waits submerged just below.

He drove through an unusually dark Mosswood then onto the I5, pushing his truck to its limit. Mariee was gone and there was nothing but death and nightmares for him on the reservation.

He arrived home in Salem just as the sun was rising. Exhaustion and grief pulled him down onto the couch. He dreamt he was flying over the ocean, the sky filled with the flapping wings of death owls. He felt sleek, like he'd grown a layer of otter's skin.

But the death owls were not birds. They were plump, albino things flopping in the dark and suddenly Levi wasn't in the air but deep underwater. He plunged into a crevasse. Into abject blackness.

Levi retreated to the center of Arizona, severed all contact with friends, family and colleagues. He threw his phone out the window somewhere along Route 95. He was resigned to the fact they'd invade the surface soon enough, and when that happened all aspirations would simply be water under the bridge.

Though he'd dropped off the grid, as far as he could tell neither the white cops nor the Coastal Colony Tribes authorities ever tried to contact him. Maybe the Rez law and those working on the excavation were in on the conspiracy—Levi didn't know and was resigned to the fact he likely never would. He read the news online at the public library to prevent anyone tracing his whereabouts. The police had launched an investigation into Dr. Alex Hardy's disappearance.

But there were no media reports concerning Adam Joseph or Mariee. Levi wasn't shocked that a missing white man attracted more attention than a vanished Duwamish teenager and a Coos woman.

There was no mention of the Blood Mound site. That clay must have been a veritable treasure trove of human remains dating as far back as the 17th century, but there wasn't even a murmur of this in the news. Levi didn't dare contact any of his former anthropologist colleagues for fear they were involved as well.

Mariee visited him in his sleep every night.

She'd hum beautiful Makah songs about "marine snow falling" and "graveyards of whale bones," her voice fading then rising in volume, only to diminish again like a radio station while driving through a canyon. Her face would glow with a joy Levi had only seen on the faces of fancy dancers after an exuberant performance.

Mariee spoke of a tsunami that was going to wash away that terrible clay Blood Mound and cover the planet in waters so black and cold it would resemble the deepest recesses of space. She pleaded with her brother to join her, to swim away and never touch the ground again.

In his sleep, his sister's skin and hair always smelled of seawater.

As the weeks passed Levi began to dream of great *Kumugwe* treading across a brackish realm, waters stagnant with decomposing salmon and human corpses. He dreamt of things pretending to be Indians, but their bodies were too small and crooked, their faces too hideous to offer any hope of kinship.

But they persisted. They prayed into his dreams through funnels whittled from whale's bone. They left messages in his head that occasionally bobbed to the surface when he was awake. These revelations often made him cry out loud.

Levi had long known that the planet was forged from strife and ancient thunder and fire, but the depths of rot became clear to him when he was a seven-year-old boy cradling a dead child while his twin sister cried for a loss she had yet to understand. The cogs of existence are oiled by sorrow; the machine produces nothing but extinction and despair.

He wondered whether it was time to tear down the gears of the old and construct something new. Historical occupations and genocide were almost banal in their familiarity—maybe he should help Mariee blot out this world. Purge the planet and reconstruct everything from a pristine slate. Enemy of my enemy.

All he could do in the meantime was wait for the waters to rise and extinguish the stars.

THIS FRAGMENTED BODY

The Doll

places the porcelain figure back in the cabinet, closes the glass door. The dolls gaze lovingly at their benefactor then shift their glassy gaze down to the sleeping boy. Their frozen lips slide into contented smiles. The child has been exhausted from a long day of swimming. His sleep is profound and unpopulated by dream. The Doll touches the boy's hair and marvels ar how soft it is. So unlike the cold, smooth surface of its own head.

Jarrod

woke up screaming. The bedroom was back-of-your-eyelids-painted-black dark. He fumbled around on the nightstand for his phone. It was 1:28 and the lack of any light source was unusual even for a blackout. The room smelled faintly of sex sweat and the intrusive stench of burnt garlic from an unknown apartment that shared their ventilation. Mark stroked Jarrod's arm, inner elbow to wrist.

"Sssshhhh. Nightmare again?"

"Mm hm."

"You ok?"

"Yeah, of course. This time they had porcelain teeth."

"Fuck that. Don't creep me out. Just a dream."

"I understand that. I'm not one of your special needs students."

Jarrod didn't mean to snap, but Mark's condescending tone set him off. He'd dealt with night terrors since he was a kid, but every once in awhile the puppet one would come back. Floppy limbed things with bathroom-sink smooth skin, cold stiff hands pinching.

Not hard, just incessant. Nibbling at the toes on his right foot like a Garra Rufa fish pedicure.

Porcelain goddamn teeth.

He was embarrassed at his crying out; nightmare or not it was still nothing but phantom pains. At 17, he'd lost his right leg up to mid-thigh. A rare osteosarcoma. Multiple surgeries on his femur, then the amputation, two-years of chemotherapy, countless follow-up surgeries. Almost three decades ago, but those ghostly pinpricks kept seeping into his dreams.

Maybe that's why he'd studied photography and sculpture. Fashioning life-sized rag dolls and mannequins then posing them in sexually explicit displays allowed him to keep the terrors at bay. He even had a pottery artist friend make him a porcelain leg and a harness to strap it to his stump. He'd taken nude photographs of himself in various positions with his mannequins and exhibited them at various galleries. He'd long acknowledged his art was overwrought, its purpose more to shock than elucidate. His had been a brief, meteoric rise to underground artist fame until his works were eventually dismissed as too derivative of Hans Bellmer. He hadn't created anything to speak of in well over a decade.

"Wanna talk about it, dollface?"

"Real funny. Go back to sleep. Power's out by the by." Jarrod was annoyed by Mark's concern. He didn't like the insinuation he was too weak to deal with a stupid dream.

They'd been together since college, so it wasn't like his nightly panic attacks were anything new. Theirs had been a head over heels type of love. Whirlwind romance and all that shit Jarrod had dreamt about when he thought he might be straight but eventually met the right guy who corrected him of that particular delusion.

He knew Mark like an extension of his own body: every nuance, every imperfection. Mark didn't care about Jarrod's disability. Called him his "Bionic Man" the first time they'd fucked, sweaty and fumbling in the college dorm room when the others were out watching a rare uncensored screening of Raymond Borde's film *Molinier*. After sex they just held each other and Mark made that electronic bionic *deh deh deh deh* sound effect and they'd both laughed and all the tension just slipped away.

But college was a long time ago. Years had slipped away, things had gone sour incrementally. Intimacy took a powder, banal stresses led to bickering, led to no holds barred fights. Jarrod became adept at punching walls, while Mark was a right poet in his petulant threats to slit his goddamn wrists if Jarrod didn't try to see the pain he was in. *His* fucking pain? Jarrod found Mark's tantrums childish. Usually responded with a *you know where the steak knives are.*

"Wake me if you want to talk." Mark's voice was monotone.

"I'm not a fucking child."

"I'm here if you need me. Just sayin'." His role in going through the motions to placate him done, Mark rolled back over. He was quietly sleeping again in just seconds.

Jarrod gently slid his portion of the sheets aside, balanced on one foot. He was disturbed by the spongy sensation of the threadbare carpet; he'd left his shoes to air out on the balcony after that evening's jog. He opened the corroded aluminum blinds just a slit. The street was a womb of darkness. Not one lamppost or store on the block had a functioning light.

He sat on the floor, grabbed his prosthetic leg near the nightstand. Socket suction tight, snug fit, pylon cold against his fingertips. Took a step, tested it under his weight out of habit. It felt right, as if the skin and muscle and bone of his leg had been redundant, an appendage he'd been born with unnecessarily.

As Jarrod walked through the bedroom doorway Mark whispered, *Please don't go outside. The children have mirrors.*

He felt susceptible standing naked in the dark room. While he'd always been the night-screamer, Mark was quite the sleep-talker. The couple had a running joke that if they ever got married they'd include "in sleeplessness and in health" with their wedding vows.

He loved Mark deeply. No question there. But they were such distinct beings he wondered how they'd stayed together for as long as they had. No denying he'd looked amazing at that Black Flag concert back in '86. Place stinking of sweaty punks, Mark the only other Black kid in a sea of shaved heads and ruddy skin. Took some brass balls to be openly queer in a scene that was all too quickly filling up with white trash and neo-Nazi dumbfucks. Even a bruiser like Jarrod had kept his attraction secret for months. Wasn't like Mark was particularly big—average height, skinny teenager, more likely to be found sitting in the library reading Carl Sagan or Octavia Butler than flailing in a mosh pit. Even guys like Darby Crash had to hide being gay. White suburban punks weren't exactly progressive minded.

Mark and Jarrod loved the scene and couldn't deny the music's allure. Or each other for that matter. At least in those days. Germ burns seemed so daring back then. Now Jarrod felt as if the scars were a humiliating reminder of his youthful romanticism.

He walked into the bathroom, slipped on a pair of shorts and a faded Bad Brains t-shirt. His hairline had slipped back even further. In just a few months. A subversive rage warmed his chest, ran up his throat like a hot filament. Might be time to shave the whole thing smooth. Least he could do was maintain his own looks in their relationship. Christ knew he hadn't pulled through on the monetary front.

Fuck it, no use agonizing over a wasted college degree and a skill set that meant at 46 he was too young to retire, but too old to go back to college and work toward a relevant education. He wiped a musty smelling washcloth across his face. Money ain't nothin' but an excuse to engage in another prolonged shouting match. The anger perked up again and he breathed deep, shoved it down. Relax. Ain't no reason to freak out over growin' old much less over domestic squabbles. No reason at all.

He was concerned about their neighbors. Lucinde Rojas in #304 was borderline senile but seemed to do ok on her own. He wasn't even sure what was wrong with the little girl Sophie in #302. Except that she was missing an arm. It struck him as odd she didn't have a prosthetic. Figured kids that age were vain about their appearance, would try to hide something like that.

Now that he thought about it Ms. Rojas and Sophie were also amputees. He was discomfited by the notion that the apartment building had cultivated a disproportionate number of limbless tenants.

Limbless tenants.

He laughed at the thought.

Just a power outage. Rojas and Sophie were probably fine, but he felt obligated to make sure. The two had been friendly to him and Mark when they'd first moved in. The only ones in the building who'd been welcoming with iced tea, pastries, and gossip about the other tenants. The only ones who hadn't muttered slurs under their breath when he passed by in the laundry room or when gathering the mail.

Jarrod maneuvered through the living room still cluttered with boxes from their relocation. He hoped renting a place in this run down apartment building was just a temporary setback until they got their shit together. Well, until he got *his* shit together.

He opened the sliding glass door that led out onto the balcony. The night was ominously quiet. Why were there no cars driving on Amaretto Street just a block away? He grabbed his keys and a flashlight then tiptoed to the bedroom to check on Mark one more time.

Mark had pulled the sheets up over his face. Just a thin arm exposed, dark and glassy like a carnelian sculpture. His proportions were odd, arms and legs drawn in towards the torso creating the illusion he inhabited less of the bed than usual. He was breathing softly, muttering something unintelligible.

Jarrod stepped out of the apartment into the hallway. The carpeted floor felt greasy under his bare foot. Pungent odors wafted at every step. The dark was like wading through syrupy ink; the fire doors normally held open by electromagnets had closed when the power had died. He felt an irrational need to keep his flashlight off, to avoid any attention. He ran his fingers along the flaking wall for guidance to Lucinde's place.

The candlelight wriggling in the space below her door meant she might still be awake. Jarrod knocked several times but Lucinde didn't answer.

Lucinde

was watching an old Benito Alazraki film on the Mexican classic movie channel when the power went out. The TV screen left a phantom image in the air. She was so startled by the impact of the emergency door closing she spilled her hot tea. She pressed her hand against her mouth. The moment her tongue touched flesh she heard a baby screaming.

She felt her way carefully to the kitchen counter for some candles and a box of matches, then slid forward incrementally, relying on the stability of her prosthetic foot, swiped her flesh and blood foot left to right for obstacles.

The candlelight softened the darkness but conjured jittery shadows. She hoped the child was with its parents; the thought of an innocent playing outside this late frightened her.

She glanced out the window. Something small and pale pranced in the middle of the street. The shape reminded her of a baptismal doll she had as a child.

Lucinde's Doll is hand sewn by her aunt. Stitched satin patterns shaping smooth cloth into a little girl with plump cotton insides and abalone shell button eyes. The doll is a baptismal gift for little Lucinde. She falls asleep with it on her chest. Breath matches doll's breath, both shudder into sleep simultaneously.

She'd passed the doll along to her daughter Maria after the baptism. Maria held onto it all through childhood, well into college. Her boyfriend Tony introduced her to heroin and violent mood swings and late night visits from the cops and trips to the emergency room. Lucinde had gained ownership of the doll again only after Tony punched Maria so hard a blood clot lodged in her brain. When she visited at the hospital she didn't recognize her Maria— her daughter's face had become the mask of an inert mannequin. Maria died 3-days later.

Shortly after the funeral Lucinde propped up the doll on the pillows of her daughter's vacant bed. It was a futile gesture, maudlin even, but it was all she had left. Over the months it seemed as if the doll's limbs filled out the sheets like a growing little girl. Its cheeks had even attained a vibrant hue.

When Lucinde was diagnosed with Alzheimer's she donated the baptismal doll and everything else that reminded her she'd once had a child of her own. But there was still a phantom indentation on the bed from the doll's weight.

Beneath her sorrow lurked an ugly current of smug piety. She'd warned Maria that the boy was no good. Tony had no job, no education, no future. A thug who wasted his days getting high with the gangs that ran in the neighborhood.

Lucinde couldn't hold back tears at her callous judgment, but the need to lash out and blame anyone other than the person responsible overwhelmed her. How could a loving God allow her precious child to die while her worthless murderer was alive and well in prison?

Surely God had guided every aspect of the tragedy, so her questioning His decisions felt immoral, blasphemous even.

She was tired from the short walk to the kitchen. She could have fallen, broken something, and then where would she be? But she was proud of herself for still remembering so much about Maria and the doll.

Several pale shapes moved in the street. She put her glasses on but the forms still seemed both startlingly small and shockingly monstrous. They danced in a disquieting manner.

She gasped when someone knocked on her door.

Jarrod
stopped knocking.

Screw it. Lucinde was probably safely asleep. Come back in the morning. He turned across the hall to #302. A faint bass beat throbbed inside. Shitty dub step music.

He knocked, cupped his hands to the door and called Sophie's name. His annoyance made him raise his voice a bit too much. He realized he sounded furious.

Sophie plucked strands of hair from her scalp. Her mom was still making weird noises in her sleep, so she turned the stereo up. She heard the security door slam then noticed that the blue numbers from the oven's clock were extinguished just before the radiance of the city's street lamps faded like heat escaping pavement at nightfall.

She stared out the black rectangle of the window and continued to methodically tug clumps of her hair out. Her mother stopped making sounds, though Sophie did hear her shift on the bed followed by a soft thump on the floor. Probably an empty wine bottle.

The prescribed antidepressants had done little to curb Sophie's trichotillomania. It wasn't fair. Most girls her age didn't live in a wasted slum, didn't have to contend with a bedridden mother and their own anxiety that compelled them to compulsively pull their own hair. And she sure as hell didn't know anyone who'd lost a goddamn arm.

She heard tiny plastic shoes clattering up and down the street. This reminded her of the time she'd wandered the hills several years ago.

Sophie is barefoot, her cheap plastic shoes have split and fallen off, but the ground is soft sand and the largest pebbles rounded by water activity years ago. The possibility of a flood rushing through the ditch raises the fear that somewhere high up in the hills a reservoir will burst its banks and sweep her away. This fear tickles her mind like the tiny stone caught between her toes.

Sophie's Doll is pressed into the dirt wall. The doll's face is a smooth pink button in the dirt, round as a teacup saucer in her doll set at home. She scrapes the dirt out of its eye sockets, rubs her thumb across the lips to reveal its elfin face flushed strawberry-pink from the intense sun.

She names him Noah because that was her father's name.

Sophie held a memory of Noah walking away down the hall of their home on Fig Street. She must have dreamt it. The doll had probably just been misplaced in one of their many moves over the last few years. Or crushed at the bottom of a box so her mother had thrown him away hoping Sophie wouldn't remember he existed.

A commotion in the street, like wisps of steam escaping a vent. Were there toddlers stumbling around out there?

Something began to scream in a voice that wasn't a child's. Sophie jumped when someone at the door growled her name.

Jarrod

spoke Sophie's name once more, softly this time. Exasperated, he slapped his palm against the wall. Something skittered in the space between the sheetrock. Powder filled his lungs.

He coughed. Hoped it wasn't some malignant mold stirred up.

The iron wrought front gate to the complex snapped shut. He heard footsteps running down the sidewalk. An anomalous sound, the *click clack* of a child wearing tap shoes sprinting across concrete.

Jarrod raced down three flights of stairs. He'd always been athletic and his prosthetic leg was state of the art, so he quickly cleared the steps. The front gate was closed. He turned his flashlight on, but the night sky blended seamlessly with the ground.

He opened the gate.

There was nobody around. It was late and a weeknight, but there should still be the hum of city life, the roar of traffic, police helicopters. Anxiety sweat coated his face. Breathing far too heavily for a man as fit as himself. Something could be lurking in the darkness just a foot or two from him, shrouded in impenetrable blackness. The thought angered him more than anything else. He felt as if someone were spying from their hiding place, mocking his inability to get to the root of whatever was going on.

The complete lack of electricity made him wonder if some bizarre atmospheric disruption had knocked out the power. Could an electromagnetic pulse cause such a widespread power outage, or was that limited to the realm of sci-fi? Mark would know about the science of it all, but Jarrod didn't and was uncomfortable with the implications.

He walked along the sidewalk, flashlight skimming the ground to prevent stepping on any shards of glass from broken bottles scavengers inevitably dropped while raiding the apartment building's dumpster. The feeling of being observed intensified as if the parties watching had increased in quantity. Something under the cover of a deep shadow hissed.

Jarrod was relieved when his flashlight's beam picked out a cat dashing across the pavement over the cinderblock wall. He was probably just being watched by several of the feral cats a well meaning but annoying tenant kept feeding. *Pussy jumping at pussies. Ha ha.*

His light's beam revealed a petite doll's shoe in front of a shrub. He picked it up, thought of that summer years ago.

Jarrod just 9, his grandfather recently felled by a stroke. Grandma had invited him and his sisters Sarah and Angela to keep her company on the ranch while school was out. A summer of playing hide and seek around the property and swimming in the lake. Months of cartoons and unhealthy food and peeled skin sunburns. Not one care to be had.

His sisters had their own guest bedroom but Jarrod had to sleep in his grandmother's doll room. He was usually too exhausted from playing all day to mind despite those frozen bisque faces smiling down from their display cases and shelves.

But some nights he'd lay wide awake and stare at the soft swath of starlight shining across synthetic hair and porcelain skin. On those nights, when he'd eventually fall asleep, he rarely remembered his dreams. Now as an adult when he dreamt it was of his sister Sarah all those years ago.

Sarah splashing in the water. Angela and Jarrod thinking she was joking so by the time he swam to her his chest felt hollow and Angela was sobbing in the shallow water but he was too scared to dive down deep into the murky depths to grab Sarah's hand. Just watched her sink deeper, staring at him with no recognition. An expressionless doll's face.

Jarrod placed the shoe back on the ground. Couldn't believe he was crying. Sorrow turned to embarrassment to anger. *Fucking weak Jarrod. Fuckin' weak.*

A light turned on in the building.

Someone was moving around in apartment #303.

The Doll
adjusts the machines. Moves the mirrors into position. Carefully arranges everything just so.

Lucinde
opened her door a crack. She couldn't imagine how the person who knocked was able to disappear so quickly.

#303's door was open. The sepia light escaping into the hall meant they had power. She heard a child's voice inside and felt an irresistible urge to be elsewhere, to escape this dreary place, push back her encroaching dementia that much longer. She knew it was irrational but she was convinced the baptismal doll was within reach.

Diabetes had reduced her to a fragile bird-like thing. No matter how aggressive her Alzheimer's had been in devouring memories she'd never forget waking up in the hospital after the surgery. One leg above the covers, a cast wrapped around her ankle that ended in a stump. Her beautiful Maria sitting next to her petting the back of her wrist as if it were a delicate newly hatched chick. She'd been mortified; she knew her skin felt like dry leaves and her face was far too old to be her daughter's mother. But she couldn't form the words to explain this.

Oh mija. Oh mija, Maria mija. Mija. My foot is in a hole. I can't find my foot. My foot is in a hole.

She wanted to tell Maria how proud she was, how much she loved her and how she wished she'd stay away from that boy who wasn't good enough. But her brain and mouth refused to cooperate. Phantom words took their place:

Oh mija. My foot is in a hole. I can't find my foot.

She'd closed her eyes to keep from crying, but when she opened them again her phantom foot felt bloated with medications, ached with surgical violence. Her daughter was gone. The only occupant in the room a black pit descending into the floor. The pit kept moaning over and over,

My foot is in a hole.

But it was just useless flesh. Something rancid that necessitated disposing of. She survived diabetes, survived the death of her child, she'd continue surviving. She crossed herself, whispered her daughter's name, blew out the candles. She left her apartment, her belongings, her life. Left everything behind.

Sophie

couldn't hear whatever was screeching on the street anymore. She looked through the peephole. There was nobody at her door.

She grabbed a flashlight from the junk drawer, cradled it under her armpit as she used her real hand to unlock and slide the latch aside. She cautiously opened the door a few inches, held it ajar with her stump, moved the flashlight around as if teasing an invisible kitten. She felt her phantom hand spread its fingers, the weight of the door against the non-existent palm. The dark seemed to impede the beam's reach though she could see that room #303 had a light on.

Sophie had been excited to see her dad that day. It had been his visitation weekend and they'd gone out for frozen yogurt. Picked her up in his battered '87 Toyota, gardening tools strewn in the back.

A drunk off-duty police officer leaving a strip club in the late afternoon cut his SUV across Carlisle St. into oncoming traffic. Side swiped the truck as her dad tried to swerve out of the way. The drunk hit the front of the Toyota, slid from dad's side diagonally until the steaming hot grille pressed against Sophie's tiny left arm, mangling it beyond any hope of recovery.

The doctors successfully performed an amputation, but her father had suffered such severe head trauma he died 30-minutes after arriving at the hospital. Sophie was 5-years old then but clearly remembered the SUV's baby seat in the middle of the road next to her father's rakes, leaf blower, plastic garbage cans. She remembered the small smile on her dad's face, temple resting against the steering wheel, black blood matting his hair to his forehead. One eye closed, the other partly open as if he were in mid-sneeze. A comical ventriloquist dummy's face.

She'd never truly missed her arm. It was like losing a tooth, and though limbs couldn't grew back in like her molars, the vacancy felt appropriate. An infection lanced by a sterile needle, the pressure of sickness relieved.

A surge of affection for her mother caused Sophie to hesitate, but she wanted to discard her decade of existence and start over. To be done with this miserable world that offered nothing to a bright 10-year old girl who just wanted everything to stop being so steeped in gray monotony and self-loathing desperation.

She wanted to escape into apartment #303.

Jarrod

navigated the stairwell back to the third floor. Something child-sized dashed across the hall. Towards #303.

"Fuck's that?"

He suddenly remembered gleaming porcelain, dresses billowing like submerged jellyfish bulbs, the clatter of tiny glass feet. Button eyes peering out of shadow.

Jarrod is certain he hears something moving around in his grandmother's doll room. His eyes adjust to the dark, a shadow quivers against the wall. A figure on the lower shelf totters, sways forward, inexplicably falls upwards onto the top shelf. This ascension fills him with horror— not the fear that the dolls will harm him but the frisson of witnessing something that should never have occurred.

He wished he wasn't standing in the hallway of a filthy apartment building, soiled carpet under his naked foot, dingy yellow walls peeling. He wanted to be that child dreaming about dolls in his grandmother's home. He wanted everything to go away and return to that time when he was tired from swimming all day and the cancer hadn't stolen his leg and he was still so deep in love anything seemed possible.

And maybe, just maybe, his sister Sarah wasn't 30-years dead.

Apartment #303 had a light on. He turned the doorknob. It was unlocked.

He'd always assumed the interior was the same for every rental in the complex, but #303's hallway seemed to extend beyond what the building's actual dimensions could allow.

He realized too late that he'd shut the door behind him. This side had no knob, no handles, no means to open it. Fear ameliorated his anger, but frustration still ached in his jaw. The only exit was a pet door built into the wall at the end. There was nowhere else to go so he crawled through.

He came out into an impossibly large room, far more expansive than the entirety of the complex's third floor. The space was illuminated by a sodium vapor lamp that cast a dull luminescence.

The floor was so heavily layered with thick rugs every footstep was muffled. Aqua-blue shag carpet lining the walls absorbed the sound of his breathing. He felt a pressure in his head, as if he'd been submerged in a diving bell. Confusion made him stumble.

Stacks of body parts were strewn about.

It took a moment for Jarrod to realize they were prosthetics: wooden legs, glass arms, porcelain torsos. Plastic heads dangling from cords like a nightmarish department store display. Synthetic limbs so tall they touched the floor and ceiling. Others as small as a toy's parts.

A table towered over him, yet paradoxically the chairs could be held in the palm of his hand. This failure to accurately interpret the proportions of the room and his own body dissolved and he felt his normal size again.

He gathered his equilibrium, walked further into the room to find the apartment building's residents supine on rusted metal tables. Strapped down by weathered leather straps, button-eyed and motionless, skin reflecting light like delicate glass figurines. They were surrounded by extraordinary machines.

More a sculptor's bizarre reconstruction of medical equipment than functional devices. Jutting pieces of metal flowered with brass panels, arms ending in mirrors like reflective fruit. A series of protrusions attached to mirrors angled just so to reflect other mirrors until ultimately reflecting a prosthetic limb, a torso, or head on display. Dozens of reflective surfaces positioned on stands, or bolted to frames that allowed the mirrors to swivel into different positions.

Lucinde was on a gurney, staring into a large mirror positioned inches from her face, angled to reflect a monstrous pair of legs propped up against a wall.

Mirrors circled Sophie. Staring at her own arm and face reflected from another mirror that received the incident ray of a small doll's arm and head. An infinite array of manipulated self assessments. A gathering of xenomiliacs seeking asylum from their misery.

The gurneys quivered, thunder rolled through the building. Powdered rust drifted to the floor, but the residents remained motionless and continued to gaze into mirrors displaying phantom childhood reflections. Something moved on the other side of the room.

The Doll

walked with a peculiar gait. Its absurdly diminutive body shrank until it was so tiny it could curl up comfortably in Jarrod's arms. The Doll's skin was pink as if freshly scrubbed.

Jarrod couldn't accept that he was standing in a strange apartment with dozens of neighbors being experimented on. Surrounded by reflections. Watching this thing fashioned from porcelain step out of his nightmares. Thunder convulsed the building. The vibrating continued even after the sound passed.

The ceiling felt too high, the floor too close. Jarrod was submerged in deep waters looking up at a sky distorted by a rippling surface. Sarah's face occluded the sun. He reached for his long dead sister. His hand brushed against her flesh, ice cold and smooth in death.

I'm done. I give up.

All he had to do was open his mouth and breathe in the past. *Give up.* But this meant he'd never see Mark ever again. A tranquil sorrow, dull and deep, numbed his anger until all that remained was longing.

The Doll's fingers gripped his wrist. It spoke in a voice coated the inside of Jarrod's skull.

All of the children have mirrors.

Jarrod

woke up in bed. The phantom memory of straps tightening across his wrists and torso gradually faded. A vague image of the Doll's head moving erratically in the gloom as it positioned a mirror before his face was all that remained of the nightmare.

The night was still ink black.

Mark was asleep. Jarrod didn't know where he'd placed his phone or flashlight. He tossed and turned trying to fall asleep again, to put the weird nightmare behind him.

The persistent *tink tink tink* of little ceramic hands tapping against the sliding glass door lulled him into a cognitive limbo.

He turned over onto his stomach, desperately clinging to the idea that if he fell asleep the power would come back on and the world would be back to normal when he woke up. His anger was distant, foreign and aloof as sorrow took its place. *Mark, I love you. I'm ok now. You mean more to me than I mean to you. It's ok now.*

The tapping grew more agitated.

This time it was Mark who began screaming in his sleep.

Jarrod reached out to comfort him. When he touched what was far too cold and porcelain-smooth to be a shoulder he realized he was having difficulty determining just where Mark was located on the bed.

The body was much too small.

The Doll
places the porcelain residents back on the shelf in Jarrod's grandmother's room. The Doll brushes their hair, straightens the silk blouses, shuts the glass door. It steps back to watch the young boy Jarrod sleeping peacefully.

TELLURIAN FAÇADE

Ian remembered the mossy cow skulls floating outside his window. The thought came to him like a vague dream, so distant yet intrusive he felt like a ghost invading the privacy of his own childhood.

But that was a lifetime ago. These days the only phantoms puttering around on the ranch took the shape of his father attired in the bones of a ruined past.

Josh and Lindsay's bedrooms remained just as he remembered. As each of them flew the coop their parents simply shut the doors and ignored the empty rooms–out of sight out of mind time capsules. He touched Josh's door, suppressed the memories that ran through his fingertips like a current. He wasn't looking forward to his siblings flying out, but their father's funeral meant a reunion could no longer be avoided. Even inside the house he smelled the sweet smoke of someone burning leaves on the other side of the mountain.

He still had dreams about swinging that hay hook into his dad's neck. All these years later he regretted that he never had the balls to wake up, sneak into his parent's bedroom, and sink that steel point into the fucker's throat. But no matter how many times he'd pulled the hook slit open, or how much blood he spilled onto the barn floor, he'd always wake up just as empty as he'd been before.

He wandered down the old familiar hall with its scratched wood paneling pocked by holes where 4-H ribbon awards had once been prominently displayed. An aggressive wind forced drizzle against the windows with a clatter. It sounded like an animal trying to get inside. Ian walked into the dining room.

The landline had been cut shortly after his father's illness. Ian didn't remember if he'd ever even seen him make a phone call. He was uncomfortable exploring his old home, anxious at the realization he was as isolated as anyone could be in this day and age.

He pressed a thumb against the tabletop, print perfectly captured in the dust as if he'd been booked.

It was early morning but the birch trees had grown so close to the house the only light came from the unobstructed window. A flipped switch gave no response.

Ian was grateful he'd held onto his dad's Vietnam Zippo. He wrangled up some candles. Their dim incandescence allowed him to read something engraved on the lighter.

NON GRATUM ANUS RODENTUM.

The autumn air made him feel like a kid again. The woods out back beckoned. He blew out the candles. Their waxy odor drowned out the scent of the distant blazing leaf pile.

Ian hiked further up the mountain, intoxicated by the scent of Douglas fir trees. Tangerine and scarlet and purple leaves tumbled over each other so he couldn't tell what was alive or animated by a breeze. Animals screamed, not quite chirps or yips. He wondered what had riled them up. His boots slipped in the mud. Every step forward was an accomplishment.

He hiked until he'd traveled deep enough to find his old underground fort. He'd spent an entire summer digging the pit and the passages branching off. Planned on reinforcing the walls, but couldn't lug cinder blocks this far. Adolescent dreams of miles of tunnels in his own underground empire, but all he'd managed was a shallow den and a few short crawlspaces. The whole system had caved in after a heavy rain, then brimmed with water that turned larvae infested.

A gnarled blackberry bush grew from the banks of the depression. Ian realized with a touch of sadness that his secret stash of Devil Dinosaur comics and Mack Bolan novels buried down there for over three decades had to be nothing but pulp now.

He gingerly pushed the thorny vines aside and found a stone wall, shin high, running alongside a tunnel split off from the foliage choked hole. It was a dark mossy green, slick from the condensation glittering like jewels on its surface. He was surprised to discover this was the natural color—no lichens grew on the marble smooth stone so tightly stacked he couldn't tell if there was any mortar. Had no idea how he could've missed the wall in all the years he'd roamed these parts.

The unusual mineral color made him think of his projectile point collection. His elementary school library had a guide that helped him become adept at differentiating a dart from an arrow tip–though his father had always insisted the ones he found on the property were thunderstones. Ian laughed at the thought; his father had also believed that animal burrows were entrances to abandoned cities.

But there'd been a knapped arrowhead he'd never managed to locate in any reference book. Made from a deep jade colored stone similar to this wall. The July he'd found it was the summer someone broke through the sliding glass door at the side of the house. Plenty of accessible rifles and trapping gear to steal, but all the bastards had taken was his projectile collection.

He pressed an ear against the wall and heard things below–watery tinkle of small stones rolling down an embankment, maybe an underground stream or lake. There were lots of subterranean reservoirs in these parts. Nez Perce had probably built this. Maybe a scrapped try at a well and geological activity had recently exposed the stones.

So much history in the forest, all kinds of wonders bound to come to the surface eventually. As his dad used to say, *Worlds buried beneath worlds.*

Terminar antes de la puesta del sol, Ambrose said as if failing to finish his chores quickly would attract the attention of something he wanted to avoid. The ranch hand had shown up later than usual. Ian was glad to see him. He'd forgotten what an integral presence he'd been growing up.

The barn had fallen into disrepair. Walls sagged, marked by cavities where horses had chewed the wood raw like poorly healed wounds. The reek of mildew and manure and a stronger odor emanated from cracks in the cement floor. Ian didn't understand how sewage had managed to leak uphill from the septic tank into the barn. He said this out loud.

Pasajes secretos. Here long before the Indios, Ambrose explained.

Passages? Ian was slightly embarrassed; his mother had been born and raised in Guanajuato, but he'd only managed to pick up a smattering of Spanish. And most of that was learned from Ambrose himself.

Abandonado burrows, conectados por lo México cuevas. Indios explore, things found down there, no le gustaba.

What'd they find? Encontrar?

Oh, ancient ceremonias. Ambrose frowned.

Cómo?

Practicante de la Vias Verdes, Tlaloc fanáticos.

Ian wasn't sure what to make of this. He rolled his thumb across his dad's vintage Zippo lighter's wheel, held it next to a fracture in the floor. The flame tip wavered towards the opening.

Ambrose's Mesoamerican fables were familiar, reminiscent of Ian's father whisking the family away to this ranch 35-plus years ago under the pretense he was saving them from conflicts in the Middle East, gas crises, and nuclear threats. Filled his kid's heads with tales about tribes that prospered in the Americas long before humans crossed the Bering Strait, of all manner of flesh and blood spirits slipping out of their intangible worlds to haunt this tangible soil.

As he'd told it certain clans used to banish their strongest braves because they were just too damned good at fighting to fit into polite society. That's how he'd seen himself—didn't belong with the nine to fives; returned from a war tour then moved his family far away from the entropy of civilization.

A real goddamn warrior.

Fanáticos, Ian agreed.

The rift in the barn floor brought to mind cenotes, sinkholes where ancient Mayans had lowered sacrificial victims into the watery depths. Ian half expected his old man to pop up from behind a rotting hay bale like a mossy jack-in-the-box.

Ambrose didn't go to the second floor. Ian was grateful for not having to make up an excuse to avoid treading up those ominous stairs where his dad had ruined everything.

Talk of tunnels inspired Ian to hike to his underground fort again. Sunlight shimmered between gaps in the cloudy sky, softly warmed the forest floor a burgundy hue.

The stone wall had ascended in the brief time he was away. He could now see petroglyphs etched into its surface. Ian estimated it was 30 feet lengthwise now. Yellow tamarack needles and alder cones were bunched around the perimeter.

Someone had started to stack stones here long ago and the lakes underfoot had moved the earth, swallowed everything, held it in its gut for ages, and now the waters were forcing the wall through the forest floor.

In a matter of hours.

This was the only scenario that made sense.

Ian placed his hands on the wall and felt something reverberating against it again and again deep below. Frenetic pummeling, rushing waters, roaring streams.

Or drumming.

That made no sense. It was water. That must be it. Subterranean rivers.

He'd come out first thing in the morning. Get some gloves. Do some measuring. Clear away those blackberry vines.

Ian began the hike back to the house. He thought the strange green sky was some weird optical illusion due to the full moon having not yet fully set. He couldn't come up with any other explanation.

Josh and Lindsay waved to get Ian's attention as he approached the luggage turnstile. His sister looked great, his brother paunchy–a barrel shaped torso gave him a bovine appearance. He'd once overheard their father say that at 14 Josh was the mental equivalent of an 8-year old. Ian wondered what mental age his 40-something brother had finally achieved.

This had stayed with him all these years, fueled his hatred of Josh as his relatives coddled and made excuses for his big brother's failures. He'd struggled for what little he had, borne the full brunt of the bankruptcy and subsequent divorce while his parents hadn't chipped in a dime. But when Josh needed help after one of his many hare-brained schemes, there'd always been a spare room or funds to help him get back on his feet.

Ian helped them gather their luggage. They stopped at the airport restaurant before hitting the road.

His brother and sister ordered food. He sipped his beer at a deliberately slow pace to show how much self-discipline he'd mustered. He was on his fourth by the time the food arrived.

You two ok sleeping in your old rooms? Not much has changed. Ian spun his coaster around in a puddle of beer glass sweat.

Not much? Albino kids still tappin' at your window? Josh snorted in amusement.

Not even a goddamn Bigfoot, though I'm expectin' one'll smell your filthy ass and come a callin'.

Hah hah. Remember when you saw kids runnin' in the woods one night? Heads all weird?

Sounds like something dad made up.

Dad didn't make things up. He knew the land.

Only reason we moved to the boonies was it made it easier for him to beat the shit outta his wife and kids without any neighbors complaining.

C'mon. He knew what was what.

Yeah, knew all about cities built before the Pleistocene. He ever tell you about the Chiricahua riding pterodactyls outta tunnels in Arizona? Bullshit. Old fool knew fuck all.

Lindsay interceded, Ian please don't use big words just so you can make yourself feel smarter than your brother. And keep it down. People are looking.

Not my words. Dad's. Remember? Hollow planet, worlds beneath worlds, all that shit? A tellurian façade?

No. I don't remember. And I don't know why you feel the need to embarrass us in public. We're going to bury our father tomorrow and this is no way to honor his memory.

Ian found it difficult to restrain an outburst with the accumulation of alcohol and anger in his belly. He almost brought up what their dad had done in the barn right then and there.

Thought better of it.

Not much was said on the long drive back to the house, though Lindsay stared out her window and remarked on how wan the setting sun looked and was that the moon up already?

Ian gripped the steering wheel, stared at the gnats swirling above the rutted road in the half-light.

Nothin' but a goddamn tellurian façade, he mumbled through clenched teeth.

Desangrado. Enfermidad nueva. Cuatro head of cattle, Ambrose said.

Head of cattle. It sounded weird to Ian, like the cows were missing their heads, while their round clumsy bodies still roamed around in the pasture.

You said they'd bled out?

Si. El Hombre Verde visito.

Cascar. Their back legs are broken. Ian made a snapping gesture.

Ambrose nodded, waved away a fat greenbottle fly.

Reses muertas, bring wrong animales down.

Bobcats did this?

No bobcats with luces en la montaña.

Lights?

Ambrose nodded emphatically, his battered cowboy hat slipped over his eyes. Linterna.

Poachers with lanterns. Ian was only half-joking.

Demasiado pequeños.

Mind taking care of it? I mean like con fuego? Torch 'em. Let the realtor and the next poor bastard worry about this shithole.

A horse whinnied long and loud. Ian helped Ambrose drag the cattle behind the barn. Flies swirled in the air, settled on the carcasses in black twitching blankets.

It was time to enter the barn's second floor. Ian's hands shook. He'd put it off too long. Couldn't stop thinking about his dad, sweat streaming off his angry face.

Ian, Lindsay and Josh had been building hay forts when their father stomped up the barn stairs.

He'd grabbed Josh by the throat, lifted him off the floor, backhanded repeatedly with a free hand. The boy had dangled there at the end of his dad's arm, oddly calm during the whole ordeal. Walleyed and accepting as if everyone had a father who disciplined with his knuckles.

Kids done messed up my bales!

Punched Josh in the chest so hard he flopped around like a mobile above an epileptic baby's crib.

Ian and Lindsay could only watch as their brother bawled, drool slick on a wet chin like a newborn calf.

Dad spun Josh to the wood floor, grabbed the belt loop on the back of his jeans. Pressed a knee into his son's spine, one hand around his throat, other holding onto the denim slipping over the boy's hips as Josh screamed for mom but they all knew she was in town grocery shopping and Ian could tell by his voice that this had happened so many times before and mom had never shown up then either.

Yanked the head back so he was staring directly at his brother and sister. All Ian could think of was how dad would put calves in a headlock and force feed them from a bottle.

He'd laughed at the sight of his brother sprawled there, jeans pulled down bare-ass for all to see, hay clinging to his snot sticky face like one of those magnetic toys with the iron filings beard.

This is funny? Their father's voice sustained rage.

No sir, Ian and Lindsay had replied in unison.

They'd left Josh behind and ran into the forest to swordfight each other with broken broom handles.

Ancient history, Ian said quietly. Water under bridges. The walls seemed to absorb his words, spat them back. He grabbed a tape measure, shovel and gloves. Hurried downstairs to the barn floor.

He wandered outside and found himself in the corral, in the precise spot he'd held the dog's legs down while his dad castrated it with nothing but a buck knife and rags soaked in hot water. He'd refused to allow Ian to name the animal; its sole purpose was to scare off whatever had been sneaking down from the mountain to steal chickens.

He'd mutilated the dog, left it to recuperate in the dirt, panting and whining in the muddy blood, testicles unceremoniously tossed nearby. The dog had survived the ordeal. Lived long enough to die years later when a spooked horse kicked him in the head.

Ian wasn't sure what he would've called the dog.

He waved to Ambrose, asked if he needed any help. He waved back and shook his head in the negative. Josh and Lindsay were probably still asleep. Ian had time to waste.

He trekked up the hill. Ran dog names through his head until he found himself at his fort again. He extended the tape measure along the stone wall to find it had risen even more. He removed the gloves, slid his hand across the sleek surface, fingertips dipping into the petroglyphs' grooves.

The bottom of the pit had fallen into a deep hole. The blackberry bushes were gone, presumably into the opening. He couldn't see the bottom. Three more knee-high wall sections had pierced the ground, surrounding the maw like rising antigorite towers.

Maybe there was a whole village beneath his feet.

He threw some branches into the gaping entrance, but felt wary as if standing before the chasm made him vulnerable. Josh and Lindsay were probably awake by now and wondering where he'd gone off to. He needed a shower.

He headed back down the mountain. The shovel, tape measure and gloves were left behind.

Ambrose had started to burn the cattle. Ian walked towards the plume of smoke darkening the sky like an appeasement blotting out the heavens.

Ian imagined his father's skin had been so weakened by age he could press his thumbprint into it. The funeral home's deep avocado walls and tobacco stain yellow curtains accentuated the room's dinginess. It seemed fitting—there was no romance to be found in death, nothing beautiful or profound. Death was as mundane as bad breath, as glamorous as clogged pores or greasy hair.

Josh and Lindsay spoke solemnly with yet another war vet he had yet to meet. Lindsay's put upon expression let Ian know how she felt about him not participating in the conversation.

He didn't care. His father had degenerated into inert particles that represented something torn down from a former glory, tarnished by what he'd become later in life. Fucking waste matter.

The veteran noticed Ian standing alone.

I'm Donald. 1st Infantry Division. What a great man we've lost.

Thanks for paying your respects.

Least I could do. A great man.

Yeah, a real warrior, Ian said.

Lindsay glanced across the funeral home in reaction to his sarcastic tone. Ian wondered if she resented anything, if she harbored the past's poisons in a secret place. He looked away from his sister and watched Josh touch the casket as if to confirm its solidity.

Ian was impatient for the service to end, though he was dreading following through on their father's request to bury the Vietnam Zippo in the forest where they'd dispersed their mother's ashes. But it had been one of the few requests in the will. That and passing the ranch on to his daughter and sons. He was obligated.

He was all for selling the war memento online to a collector. When he'd mentioned this to Lindsay she'd accused him of being intentionally hurtful. He hadn't told her she should be used to intentional harm.

Josh scooped a shallow grave in the soft dirt. Lindsay reverently placed the Zippo in the hole, pushed soil back over it, stamped it down.

She said a prayer.

Josh's head nodded like a child doing their best to appear respectful as he wiped his muddy palms against his slacks. Ian kept glancing into the woods, wanting this all to end so he could get back to the house and the alcohol.

As they turned to head back he glimpsed a diminutive figure up on the hill moving its arms as if to catch his eye, or maybe warn him away. It was too blurry to make anything out at this distance, so he may have been waving back to a small shrub in the wind when his gaze shifted to movement in a copse of golden aspen their leaves blazing in the sunlight.

He looked back. There was no figure or foliage or anything there at all.

Ian poured Lindsay and Josh each a scotch. He was on his fifth. The dining room window gave a beautiful view of the pasture.

Went into the barn this morning, he said.

Everyone makes mistakes. Lindsay was infuriatingly calm.

Mom having kids with that sumbitch was a mistake.

Still our father, Josh said.

Ian was frustrated by his sister's refusal to back him up, infuriated by Josh's dim witted complacency. His temper flared.

Josh. He put you in the fucking hospital.

No business bein' in the barn. Josh whispered as if afraid their father was listening behind one of the bedroom doors.

Did things to us. Not just talkin' the barn here.

Still our father, Josh spoke lovingly, as if their agony had been of necessity.

That tone. That oblivious grin.

Ian loathed his brother more than anything at that moment. He was repulsed by Josh's weakness.

Sickened by his degradation.

Still our father. Josh repeated.

Rage suffused Ian's body, triggered him to react without thought. He swung at his big brother's moronic face, fist landing on the left temple punch after punch.

The louder Josh shrieked the more Ian hoped that helpless child suffered terribly at the hands of their father. Thick ropes of phlegmy blood gushed across Josh's cheeks.

Lindsay pulled Ian away.

His fury made everything grainy and momentarily sapped his memory. He stormed out of the house.

He found himself standing on the second floor of the barn.

Ian sat upright at the sensation of moist breath on his face. He'd fallen asleep on a pile of damp horse blankets. It'd only been a short time; there was still daylight.

He looked around, but the barn was empty.

He walked back to the house. Josh and Lindsay were gone. Ambrose must have given them a ride into town to book a hotel. The remains of a broken bottle of scotch on the kitchen floor suggested the drama had continued without him. Ian wondered why they'd left their luggage behind. Someone had tracked clumps of sopping moss all over the house.

He sat down at the table, looked out the dining room window at the pasture's borders defined by clusters of dogwood trees truncated by a shallow crick just beginning to swell dangerously high as winter encroached, narrow one-lane blacktop road interrupted by a rickety bridge county taxes had long neglected, light and air performed their alchemy, transformed the creek water and bronzed the leaves and the driveway's wet gravel into gleaming metals, the landscape coppery from a sun that was taking its sweet time to set.

He cried, sticky tears and mucous running down his chin. Just like Josh.

Jasper. My dog's name is Jasper.

Solitude gave him free reign to continue drinking, so he did just that.

Ian woke beneath a green sky. He was on the forest floor next to the pit. The shovel and gloves and tape measure were near. He threw his empty bottle of scotch into the hole. It took far too long before it struck a surface. He was startled to hear a splash as it sank into deep waters.

His legs wouldn't work.

Several malachite buildings now stood.

Monoliths risen from their graves, the original walls nearly attaining their former glory in witness to the birth pangs of an ancient city. This made so little sense to Ian he could only focus on what he assumed was a decayed stump that looked like a warrior crouching. The spear resting on the misshapen shoulder must have been an errant branch. A slab of moss covered bark peeling away gave it a cow-skull profile.

The moon was massive, the morning sun effete compared to its companion's illumination. The lunar mass moved far too quickly, like a theatrical prop pushed over the crest, sailing into the sky, hovering, a giant's idiot face projecting a magnificent verdigris glow over everything as it swelled to such a size it revealed the dark areas as mossy patches.

The moon's surface was covered in petroglyphs.

Ian's legs wouldn't respond.

He pulled himself hand over fist across the ground's crust as fragile as his dead father's skin, over unseen realms connected by hidden arteries deep beneath. The weird moon's light revealed stone stairs leading down into the pit, narrow and steep, chiseled for something much smaller than himself.

A bird called somewhere in that viridian-stone city. It sounded an awful lot like Josh screaming, then Lindsay, sometimes far away, sometimes close. Sometimes as if it were emanating from within the pit but the clatter of loose dirt falling into the opening was probably just an animal scrabbling down there. The hole groaned with the rumble of fast moving water.

I hurt my legs Lindsay! Please help me! I'm so sorry Josh! Ian shouted with no reason to think anyone was within earshot. Even so, he found the exhalation of profound silence far more disconcerting than if an ominous voice had responded.

His gaze was caught by a metallic gleam on the step, just above the point a rising tide of darkness swallowed the stairs.

He stretched his arm out to the shining object.

It was the only thing that mattered to him at that very moment. Memories of cenotes and ritual victims sacrificed to the planet's dank seeping depths trickled through his brain. But this was his. He leaned in so close his head passed the edge of the hole.

Something way down deep was running up the stairs.

Ian extended his fingers as far as he could. The pounding footfalls grew louder.

This was all he had left, the only evidence he could hold that proved his father had once been worthy of his mother's love.

He reached into the dark dribbling up his wrist until he could no longer see his hand just a hair's breadth away from the glinting artifact.

Several more footsteps joined in. The ground quaked with a proliferation of activity.

Ian's fingers closed over the cold surface of his father's Zippo lighter just as the first shape detached itself from the darkness below.

FILM MAUDIT

"The art of film can only really exist through a highly organized betrayal of reality."

-François Truffaut

Leslie had memorized the entirety of Human Wreckage's stock, from the piles of dusty bootlegs and stacks of Eurosleaze exploitation, to the *cinéma vérité* haphazardly shelved. The store's walls were papered with posters of rare or lost films. He was particularly fond of a ghastly yellow print depicting a smiling young woman holding a trephine drill poised just above her shaved scalp.

"You're a horror guy, right?" Paula looked up from counting her till. She only engaged in conversation with Leslie due to their mutual interest in film. His incessant loitering around her business and refusal to purchase anything made her reluctant to open the store every morning.

Leslie nodded, continued reading the description on a Japanese VHS import of *An Orgy of Entrails*.

"Someone dropped these off this morning." Paula held up a handful of black and white photocopies. They depicted a movie screen, a jumble of women's heads and naked torsos stacked on the stage below. The film titles were printed in tiny cramped letters, difficult to read on the cheap reproduction. Leslie was only able to make out *Lust of the Vampiress, Slit Slut,* and something that may have been *Doll Humiliation*. The date and show times were listed just above the event's name: *ABATTOIRFEST*.

"Film festival?"

"Looks like it. Mostly Euroschlock, giallo shit, buncha horror

directors I haven't even heard of. You know Aquino, McBride—"
Paula snorted in amusement. "Van Riesen?"

Leslie had to reluctantly admit he didn't. His gaze moved down
the page, snagged on one title.

Film Maudit.

He knew as much as there was to be known about *Film Maudit*.
Its writer, director, and producer were anonymous—rumor was it
may have been a collective of filmmakers. Shot in Germany, or at
least the unidentified actors spoke oddly accented German, and
released in the summer of '74 for one weekend in just a handful of
showings where it was swiftly condemned for its disturbing violence
and sexual content. All known prints had long been misplaced or
destroyed. Little else was known about the film's production. The
holy grail of lost films.

The mysterious producers had even gone so far as to hire extras
to protest outside of showings, waving signs and chanting slogans
condemning the film's alleged use of actual snuff footage. This
attempt to manipulate the viewing public had the desired effect; an
obscure foreign horror flick became a newsworthy sensation for
several days until Nixon's resignation pushed the story aside.

"Lookit." Paula tapped the page in Leslie's hand. "They even dug
up one of those Tingler machines."

Leslie looked at the ad again. An asterisk hovered next to *Film
Maudit* like a tiny puckered black star. His gaze lowered to the other
dim star fallen to the bottom of the page. The precise, calligraphic
print read: *FeatuRing A RestoRed OSCILLATOR!*

"It's not the Tingler." His heart raced. "Really? Swore I read
'Tingler'."

Human Wreckage was muggy inside, sweat dotted Leslie's face.
He ran a slick palm across his dreads.

"Kinda like the Tingler. Oscillator was more like, uh, like
'Sensurround'. Sound system used for the disaster flick *Earthquake*. So
loud it rattled the whole place."

Paula raised a pierced eyebrow. "Films were something else back
then. Who needs character development, *mise-en-scène*, narrative,
camera placement." She held her forefingers together, thumbs
straight out to form a square, framing Leslie's head in a shot.

He didn't acknowledge Paula's sarcasm. "Gimmicks ended

around the time of Water's *Polyester*. With those scratch 'n' sniff cards. Actually, now that I think about it, Gaspar Noe used something like the Oscillator. In *Irreversible*. Played a really low 28Hz frequency background sound that was supposed to disorient the audience. You know, make them sick to the stomach. Dizzy and shit. Oscillator did something like that too, but more psychedelic, like those CIA programs blasting the public with high frequency sound waves. Incapacitate the central nervous system, make the enemy hallucinate, wig out." Leslie wiggled his fingers in the air to emphasize his point.

Paula folded her arms across her chest. "Not my idea of a good movie night."

"*Film Maudit* wasn't supposed to be entertainment, it was supposed to be an ordeal. The Oscillator was gonna change the way people watched film, like actually physically fuck them up. Everyone was gonna be altered. Not just because of the sound, but the environment, the experience itself."

Paula leaned back against the counter. "You ever see *Through a Glass Darkly*? Great use of sound. The scene with the roar of the helicopter's engine triggering Harriet Andersson's breakdown. Damn. What a performance. Film has its own language. Like how we know what it sounds like when someone gets punched in the face, but it's a completely different sound when it happens in a movie. Its own way of communicating the five senses, different than real life."

"What's the gore like?"

"What? It's Bergman. You do know there's more to films than tits and blood, right?"

Leslie stroked his chin in faux contemplation. "Maybe. Anyway, so few people saw *Film Maudit* there's not much to go on. The handful of critics that 'went to a screening refused to describe the plot. Just wrote shit about it, tore it to shreds. Even accused the theater employees of slipping acid into their RCs."

Paula laughed. "LSD. Now that's a gimmick Castle never tried." She gestured towards the sheet. "Festival is at the Old Klein Theater on Boroughs Street. No idea that place was still around."

Leslie was just ten years old when he'd seen his first film unattended at the Klein. *Sorority Bloodbath*. The gruesome makeup effects, gratuitous nudity and vestigial plot led to his love of underground films, the filthier the better. Last he'd heard the theater had closed down and became a refuge for the city's booming junkie population. He hadn't heard they'd renovated and reopened.

"Supposed to spend time with my daughter that weekend, but I think I can talk her mom into watching her. I deserve some me time, right?"

"Askin' the wrong person."

"You going?"

"No can do. Burman is coming to the store that night with the lead to do a signing for *Craniofacial Holocaust.* Don't expect a big turnout, but there are some hardcore gorehounds that'll waste some time talking to the director. Who knows, one of the little leeches might actually buy something."

Leslie should have been excited he was on the way to *Abattoirfest*, but he was still fuming over his daughter's inability to do even the most basic chores around the apartment. He was tempted to just stay on the bus until it took him away from this ugly city, away from Samantha and a girlfriend who constantly made excuses for their kid's problems. Away from an existence that drained him that much more each day and replaced the void with the realization the best life had to offer had long passed. Sure he'd overreacted—but it wasn't his fault. For Christ's sake, Samantha was fourteen now. He didn't care if her delayed development was a challenge; she'd enough brains to know not to piss herself again.

The bus passed through dilapidated neighborhoods. He hated to waste fare on a ride to the Klein but he couldn't afford another DUI. The graffiti streaked windows presented a haggard man. Gray dreadlocks, red furrows of razor irritation, four-day old stubble on his cheeks like smears of ash. His reflection looked like a battered thaumatrope, face intermittently broken by the dim streetlights.

The driver pulled into a part of town where starlight slid off pale concrete and bounced from cracked glass at just the right angle to paint the buildings a tarnished lead hue. What little color remained oozed from malfunctioning traffic lights throbbing red.

The bus groaned to a stop.

Leslie walked a block until he saw the Klein Theater's sign. Pieces had fallen away, the paint had long faded. It now spelled LEIN EATER but still mimicked an old fashioned clapboard. He was giddy with anticipation. All the stress over his disabled daughter was pushed aside even if only briefly.

Some of Leslie's fondest childhood memories had been spent at the Klein. His father's drinking problem had been a mixed blessing as it initiated the weekend ritual of getting dropped off at the old movie theater, but also meant a ride home would only return after running tabs at every bar in town. But it was all worth it; the physical abuse and any lingering emotional misery had long been dulled by the wide array of weird films he'd been lucky enough to experience. The Klein used to be a place where he could dream, a refuge from the reality of a shattered home.

He wondered why there were so few cars in the parking lot.

The hand written message in the box office window read *ABATTOIRFEST Friday, Nov. 13th*. The ticket booth was vacant. He cupped his hands over the glass. What little could be seen inside was due to the wan glow of the heat bulb in a vacant popcorn machine.

Three of the four theaters had film titles posted but Leslie couldn't make them out. The theater door with no title above was larger than the others. An employee must be sweeping in the lobby— why else would anything be shuffling around in the darkened interior?

He was startled to see an arm splayed on the floor palm up, the rest of the puffy limb obscured by shadow.

He pressed his face against the window. It was just a crimson velvet rope strung to a floor stanchion that had toppled over. He wiped his sour breath from the glass and hit his knuckles gently against the window.

"Anybody home?"

A greasy palm print and the glass quivering from his tapping created the illusion of something thin falling to the floor. It crawled behind the concessions. But there was nothing alive in there; only shadows moving about like wisps of water-thinned blood swirling into drains. The place was empty.

Maybe there was another entrance or an employee outside. He walked around the corner of the building into the long alley that ran between the theater and a boarded up warehouse. The flickering EXIT sign lit up the grimy brick walls of the dead end. Something was piled several feet high just outside the door.

It looked like a stack of discarded mannequin parts. Leslie

thought it was probably a promotional display staff had dumped out back for the trash truck. Several pieces were battered and missing bits. It was only the stuttering light that made it seem as if one of the hands was swaying back and forth in greeting. He walked out of the alley as fast as he could anyway.

He was about to return to the bus stop when a dim light turned on inside the theater lobby. An old woman was standing at attention in the ticket booth. The illumination stained her skin the color of pewter.

"I was worried the festival had been cancelled," Leslie said good naturedly.

The old woman didn't respond.

"One for *Abattoirfest.*" Binge drinking over the last few hours made Leslie's inflection come across as more demanding than intended.

The woman didn't acknowledge his presence.

"So they actually got an Oscillator up and runnin'?"

The geriatric's hands shot through the gap, closed on Leslie's wrist with a jaw-trap grip, pulled his hand through the partition's small opening. Fingers scraped against glass. She stamped the back of his hand with an image of the theater's clapboard logo.

"Shit, thanks a lot."

The money sat untouched.

As Leslie walked into the lobby he glanced back at the booth but quickly looked away; the ticket seller's posture suggested something lumpy and dusty had occupied her theater uniform.

He sucked at his bloodied knuckle. The concession stand was closed. Judging by the black grease stains on the counters and rotting patches of carpeted floor it didn't look like food or beverages had been sold here in quite some time. He was ok with that though; his stomach roiled from the nauseous combination of blood and alcohol.

Movie posters curled from the walls, stiff like dried skin. He wondered how bad this place must've looked before the renovation.

Theater #1 was showing *The Raped Void*, #2 *Screaming Throat*. Leslie wasn't familiar with either film. The third displayed *Lust of the Vampiress*—he recognized this one from the flier. He was curious about the larger unmarked theater. Probably a storage warehouse. He heard activity within, the clank of machinery. Maybe they were setting up the Oscillator. He walked into the *Lust of the Vampiress* theater.

The seats were a plush burgundy and surprisingly elegant. Dust wafted from the fabric. He stifled a sneeze so as not to annoy the handful of patrons, though they seemed captivated by the blank screen and made no move to acknowledge his presence. He wasn't too surprised at the small audience as even he was unfamiliar with many of the movies advertised tonight. But he was here for *Film Maudit*. Everything else was filler.

Movement caught his eye. He glanced up at the ceiling. Several panels were missing, their vacant squares dark and ominous as the entrance to an abandoned house's attic. He turned his whole body around to look to the projection room, hoping to catch a glimpse of the Oscillator being prepared, or even any evidence such a device existed and wasn't simply an invention to draw ticket sales. There was nothing but the dark window.

He realized he didn't have any idea what an Oscillator even looked like. He had an image of something robotic and menacing squatting next to the projector. Or maybe several small units placed in each dark corner of the theater.

The lights lowered, the projector's beam shot across the room like a lighthouse beacon. *Lust of the Vampiress* started.

Thirty minutes in Leslie chalked it up as yet another soft core Euro-thriller full of buxom undead girls in diaphanous nightgowns. The superior cinematography would appeal to the art film crowd, but he saw little else of worth. He'd seen it all before and done much better by the likes of Jean Rollins.

Then the lesbian vampires started doing something to each other he didn't find particularly erotic. Their gestures were overwrought, there was far too much chocolate sauce colored blood on the voluptuous actress' thighs. Something lying just beneath the soundtrack's surface suggested breaking glass or rust forming. Leslie found himself looking away twice. On the third occasion he confronted the screen with his gaze, but something in his peripheral vision needled him for attention.

He was frustrated with his childishness. He wasn't some kid peeking between his fingers at an actor in a rubber suit stalking some damsel in distress. He'd managed to sit through crush films and even a snuff flick he thought might be legitimately illegal. This was nothing.

One of the viewers in the front row began wriggling in their seat, tilted his head back and moaned loudly. Leslie tried to ignore the pervert and concentrate on the rest of the movie.

Had the staff activated the Oscillator? He hadn't seen anyone working here other than the old woman in the ticket booth. But he was sweating profusely, a nervous knot clenched in his gut. He had no idea why anyone would have started the device during this film though—he'd assumed it was for *Film Maudit* only. Maybe someone had accidentally thrown the switch?

Something slithered low near the bottom row. It moved with a muscular grace, like a python wrapping itself around a branch, reflecting a gray moist hide. Leslie pushed himself up in his chair, peered into the gloom. Just a glistening stain and erratic light worming across the floor.

The next feature started immediately.

Filmed in FANTASCOPE flashed on the screen. Music swelled as MDCCCCLXXXVII was followed by a crude hand drawn intertitle:

THE LATEST IN BLOOD AND GUTS

The soundtrack erupted with a chorus of unfamiliar animal cries spiraling into screams. A menagerie of species Leslie didn't recognize paraded across the screen.

He'd once read an essay on Edison's *Electrocuting An Elephant*, but this was far more horrific. How the filmmaker managed to incite the creatures to do such things to each other was baffling; even a starved beast wouldn't inflict such hideous acts in such an imaginative manner. He couldn't believe that what he was watching wasn't some elaborate visual effect. But the film was far too old to deceive with sophisticated digital tricks.

The Latest In Blood and Guts ended with no credits. Leslie assumed there'd be a break now so he stood up with the intention of using the bathroom. If it wasn't the Oscillator churning his guts it must've been the alcohol. But the next film began right away. He sat back down, crossed his legs to alleviate the pressure on his bladder and bowels.

Several more films were screened. Alcohol must have dulled his memory; he was hard pressed to remember the names of any he'd just seen much less plot details. He wasn't sure how much longer he could remain seated.

Finally, *Film Maudit* began.

Leslie clapped but stopped when someone a few seats down turned to glare at him. He thought it was cool that some horror fans were so devoted they'd dress up in grotesque masks even for a small festival like this.

He tensed. Listened for any auditory cues, a blinking light in the dark, a change in the air. Nothing. But they must have activated the Oscillator— why else would the aisle seats seem to be undulating like waves?

Film Maudit opened with a medium shot of a dirt floor surrounded by three concrete walls, the fourth removed for the camera crew. An uncomfortably young looking girl sat in the center of the room. She was naked and kneeling, face covered by a mauve paper butterfly mask. Her arms and stomach were wet with fake blood that looked like the melted-crayon waxy gore in *Profondo Rosso*.

The girl's skin, her mouth, the way she moved—all seemed hauntingly familiar.

She slowly stood.

Her waist was impossibly narrow, tapered to a wasp-thin shape. The soundtrack was just the swish of limbs against wet skin. Cries spilled from the speakers. The tension was nearly unbearable.

She walked towards the camera.

The girl's breathing didn't match her sobs. The screen filled with her face and plump crayon-red lips. She broke into a smile that threatened to become beatific. Her lush mouth dominated the theater. The soundtrack's crumbling stone sound vibrated the room.

Her knees were bent the wrong way.

The film must have been missing a reel; she suddenly appeared in another room with several other actors, all sitting cross-legged on a dirt floor. Everyone wore butterfly masks but nothing else. An intertitle read:

Sex-Welle!
Sex-Welle!
Sex-Welle!

Leslie found the makeup effects disturbing but not particularly convincing (especially that hyper-saturated blood). He thought the mutilation of the actor's genitalia was amateurish prosthetic work, but their horrified reactions made him queasy. Not bad for such a low budget sleazefest.

The audience sat completely motionless, slumped at awkward angles in their plush seats. The masturbator was mewling in what Leslie thought was prelude to orgasm. On listening further it sounded more like the panicked cry of someone too deeply submerged in nightmare to wake up.

If the Oscillator hadn't been on before it must be operational now. A growl reverberated, rattled Leslie's chest, spread through his muscles.

The theater walls felt as if they were closing in. *Film Maudit* was off somehow, the frame rate wrong. Leslie still had to use the bathroom. He needed to talk to management, request they turn off the Oscillator. That should clear things up.

He stumbled up the aisle. Couldn't believe he was taking a break from a film he'd always dreamt of seeing. But his head was filled with a strange soundtrack, the chattering susurrus of an unseen ensemble. It felt as if his brain was pulsing against his skull.

He had to get some fresh air. Had to get away from the radius of that Oscillator fucking with his head. He couldn't have been the only one to complain about the machine.

The lobby was empty. The old woman in the ticket booth was gone.

A loud knocking emanated from inside the unmarked theater. The gibbering music in Leslie's head made him retch.

The theater door shook. Something within made the sound of oily plastic sliding against rusty metal, the clank of gears and a moaning like blowing into a bottle.

Someone frantically pummeled against the other side of the door.

Leslie took a step away but not quick enough to avoid the door striking him in the face. Metal hinges tore, a stray screw sailed across the room, pinged off the ticket booth's glass. He collapsed, cheek and chin pressed so forcefully against the filthy carpet he no longer looked like himself.

An impossibly thin figure stood just inside the theater. Its form subtly distorted, not bilaterally symmetrical, like a poorly constructed clay model, one side drooping lower than the other. The screen behind it glowed with an otherworldly haze. Atavistic images caroused up there. Odd animals frolicked. Clucked and chittered and brachiated and crawled in a sinuous manner with difficult to define limbs.

A little girl stepped into frame from the right. Her face was shiny. Leslie couldn't explain why he knew she was slathered in lard much less why he was certain he'd seen those cheekbones and eyes before.

Something released itself from a phlegm-colored edge fog at frame left. It lovingly coiled itself onto the girl's face, in a precise shape, like a carefully applied swirl of feces. She was silent as several other weird predators joined in to rend her features anonymous.

Leslie was screaming so loudly he tasted blood from his raw throat.

The person towering over him was far too tall to be anything but a distorted shadow. He'd suffered a concussion. The contours of the man's face were wrong; Leslie couldn't fully comprehend what he was looking at. A concussion.

It hunched to pass through the doorway.

Head of amber, a gelatinous sculpture, special effects prop used for exploding headshots in gory film scenes. Far too many narrow limbs propelled it in one long stride until its make-up effect face was touching Leslie's face.

Invisible bodies press against him, slide over his skin with the texture of tangled kelp bulbs washing over a drowning victim as he sinks into unconsciousness.

Leslie woke up back in his theater chair. The Oscillator's music roared. The seats were now all occupied, the audience clapping and whistling enthusiastically. A remarkably skinny form sat next to him, but he couldn't turn his head to see who it was. It didn't matter much; his attention was fixed on the bizarre antics projected onscreen and he couldn't imagine why he'd want to look at anything else.

The thin companion touched Leslie's forehead with a long finger. Carved out a perfectly smooth circle, plucked the bone coin away. Poked its finger through the skull into the hole.

Exposed to the air, the film's colors bled into Leslie's fevered brain, the hue of deformed peacocks glass-tailed and shimmering. The projector's light revealed crevices in the screen. Leslie remembered a book on caves he'd treasured as a child. It had the most beautiful full-page pictures of speleothem in ancient caverns.

Film Maudit's third act. Something with far too many tongues smeared its saliva across an expanse of hairless flesh stretched taut across a room. The camera panned up its length to a pair of swollen eyes framed by a mauve butterfly mask.

The audience hooted and screeched, wriggled in their seats with excitement. Upright ticks, starved bags of viscera adorned with hair and teeth clamoring at the screen for nourishment. They turned their far too large heads towards the rear of the theater and siphoned the projector's light into mouths as dark as a changeover cue.

The Oscillator's drone masked all other sounds. The dark filled with colors both wonderful and impossible. The wound in Leslie's head slurped more light into its depths.

He could truly see now, true sight finally recognizing those eyes on the screen.

An intertitle appeared:

The streets grow active with feral hunger.

"Stop the film please." Leslie whimpered.

After Samantha had failed to develop normally, Leslie quickly realized that watching a loved one suffer the pangs of existence would slowly destroy him as well. It wasn't his fault she'd never have a normal life, it wasn't his choice to be saddled with the responsibility for a girl that would never read a book without assistance, drive a car, or graduate from college.

He knew he was selfish and petty and abusive, but existence was all that and more. The universe wasn't apathetic, it simply had an obscene sense of humor and Leslie was the victim of a genetic pratfall he'd named Samantha.

You can turn the Oscillator off now. I don't wanna see everything any more.

The final intertitle flashed on the screen:

Scavengers scurry from the sewers to lap at the wet afterbirth of night.

I don't wanna dream anymore please.

He prayed the reel would change but he knew it never would. As Samantha's eyes filled the screen the camera pressed in with a zolly shot. A phosphorous-white light filled Leslie's vision. A light as harsh and raw as peeled stars flooded the theatre.

A PLAGUE OF NAKED MOVIE STARS

Vince woke from his nightmare yet his body still felt as if it were descending into tar black sewage. His hand was lodged inside something warm and wet. An impossibly wide mouth.

"Happy Halloween, loser!" The room exploded with light, went dark, lit up again as Jason kept twisting the dimmer switch. Vince's eyes slowly adjusted until he saw that the mouth was just a plastic trick-or-treat pumpkin pail filled with tepid water. It took a few moments more for him to remember who and where he was. Adam and Jason were both out of breath from laughing.

"Yeah, classic one, dumbass." Vince slapped the pumpkin. Water splashed over the edge. His eyeballs must still be sticky with sleep; Jason *was* tall but his head shouldn't be scraping the ceiling at that unusual angle.

Adam started to sop up the water with his dirty Mercyful Fate t-shirt. "You retards gonna help me clean up?"

"Depends. We still checkin' out the Satanic murder house?" Jason flashed devil horns with both hands.

Vince still felt nauseated from all the candy he'd eaten. He'd taken a nap in an attempt to recuperate. He was dying to go with his friends to the Stanton place, but he knew he should've gone home after their day of pranking and treat pilfering. The last thing he wanted to do on Halloween night was check out the crime scene where Mr. Stanton had slaughtered his family in some sort of occult ritual.

The only reason he'd agree to spend the weekend at Adam's house was because this had likely been his last chance to gorge on chocolate and run around town knocking over stranger's witchy decorations. By this time next year he'd be far too old to engage in such juvenile stunts. "I'm out. Stomach's killin' me. I'll stay and watch TV or something."

"Strawberry Shortcake on this late?" Jason taunted.

Vince didn't want his friends to notice how rattled he was from his nightmare.

(Robed figures dancing around a twig shrine held together by mud and manure, plaster Virgin Mary statue perched at the top. Faded indigo robes, chipped hands clasped in prayer, flaking bright blue serpent under her heel. Stars shedding skin revealing brighter stars)

He didn't acknowledge Jason's taunt, just closed Adam's bedroom door behind him without a word.

Earlier that evening, after returning from their vandalism spree in Cottage Hollow, the three boys had enjoyed a marathon horror movie run starting with City of Corpses, and wrapped up with the Treehouse Massacre trilogy. Afterwards, Adam insisted they watch several religious tapes from his dad's VHS library. They'd endured 90-minutes of fire and brimstone homilies warning about human sacrifices, ritualistic torture and cult conspiracies. Satanic cult crimes were no laughing matter to Adam, but Jason found the whole thing hilarious.

Though the Christian propaganda had taken a toll on Vince's sleep, he was ambivalent as to the plausibility of the accusations. While all too familiar with Adam's rants about backmasked subliminal messages in black metal, the dangers of Dungeons & Dragons, and warlocks kidnapping sacrificial virgins on Halloween night, he also thought most of the claims were urban legends at best, pious lies at worst. But Adam insisted that role-playing games and music were all precursors to the Satanic takeover, dark covens plots to weaken the populace with psychological warfare through occult propaganda hidden in pop culture, or blatantly offered up on a sacrificial tray.

As stupid as the whole thing was, the cult stories were still responsible for some brutal nightmares.

(Devil worshippers puking streams of black blood onto the shrine, wet dirt soaking up the vomit as if famished. Stars defecating sickly blue light across the planet)

Just thinking about it forced stomach acid to the back of Vince's throat.

He was surprised Adam's devout parents were ok with their son's love of horror films and role-playing games. As long as Vince had been friends with Adam his parents had always condemned such things as filth, derided it as a testament to the moral decay corrupting the country. They'd often quoted Zephaniah 3:3 as an example of how a once Godly nation was well on its way to becoming an open sewer if they stayed on the path they were on.

But something had changed in the last couple of Halloweens; Adam's parents gone all out on the 31st. Now jack-o'-lanterns and rubber bats and plastic skull decorations peeked from every nook and cranny of the house. They'd even let Adam dress up last year.

Vince didn't get it— sometimes people held beliefs that dictated one thing, but acted in ways completely contrary. Very little made much sense to him lately.

He turned on the TV. The snow-filled screen meant the satellite dish was down so he wouldn't be able to watch the latest episode of *The Master*. There went his weekly dose of Lee Van Cleef's stunt double kicking ass.

He dragged out Adam's Intellivision, slid a laminated sheet over the controller's keypad. He couldn't help but smile when he remembered how Adam thought that even video games had mind altering subliminal messages.

He pushed the *Treasure of Tarmin* cartridge into the console and began slaying skeletons.

"Good to go Jas'?" Adam asked.

Jason turned the dimmer knob down to darken the bedroom. "More than ready. I brought my weapon." He pulled a lightsaber out of his backpack, flipped the switch as the plastic blade lengthened like a telescope. He waved the toy in circles, a zigzag of red light slicing the gloom like a cigarette tip in a dark bar.

"Wasn't that for your costume last year?"

"Yeah. Your point?"

"C'mon Jas'. Someone might see our flashlights. That'll stand out even more."

Jason sighed. "Gay in this one, the Force is." He collapsed the saber and wedged it into his back pocket.

"This is illegal as hell right? Like tampering with evidence or something?" Adam was usually the first of the gang to agree to some stupid stunt, and the one who invested the most effort into following through. But he also second-guessed every detail, eagerness to impress friends tempered by cowardice. He couldn't even explain why he'd let Jason talk him into hiking to the Stanton house on this night of all nights, when his mom and older sister were out with friends and his dad stuck doing a late shift. On Halloween. That time when the tenuous skin between the dead and the living was weakest. Adam took a deep breath to calm himself.

Jason playfully smacked Adam's arm. "Easy there Short Round. Newspapers said Stanton just hacked his wife apart. Place was full a black magic shit. Buncha Crowley and Anton LaVey books. No way I'm not checkin' it out."

"Since when did you read?"

"Hilarious. My dad's buddy works at the Cottage Hollow Review. Said the house is all boarded up but the cops do drive-bys to check for trespassers. Like twice a day. We'd see their headlights long before they got close enough to see us."

"Yeah?"

"Yeah. And my dad's buddy also said that Stanton slit his own throat."

"That's sick."

"Just sayin'. His daughter is still missing too. They only found Stanton and his wife. She had all sorts of weird symbols carved into her skin. Also found the linoleum knife that did the deed. And get this…," Jason lowered his voice conspiratorially, "*both of the bodies were naked.*"

Adam was bothered by Jason's enthusiasm. He thought about his sister Dana or his mom being brutalized and it made him furious that his friend seemed so callous about the violence.

But he was also drawn to the salacious aspects of the murders. It didn't matter if the ritual mutilations were true or fabricated tales picked up at school; he was filled with an inexplicable need to contribute to the conversation, a secret desire like his growing collection of adult magazines hidden in the slit of his mattress. It was a compulsion he found increasingly mortifying in light of his faith. "I heard Stanton drew a pentagram on the walls in blood and there were astronomy books all over his house."

"You mean astrology genius." Jason rolled his eyes.

"No. Astronomy."

"Stanton was a Jesus freak. Wonder why he snapped like that."

"Two words: demonic possession."

"A demon? You actually believe that crap?"

"I do because it's true. Hear about that pre-school in California? They molested the kids. Made them worship something in the tunnels under the principal's office. Demons made them do it."

"Oh yeah. Didn't they take nude pictures, played some perverted game?" Jason asked more to rile Adam than out of any genuine curiosity.

"*The Naked Movie Star* game!" Adam's face was bright red, whether from embarrassment or excitement, Jason couldn't tell.

"Did you hear about how the cops found nudie Polaroids of Stanton's daughter?" Jason mimed taking a photo of Adam.

"You're messed up."

Jason shrugged. "And you're way too into Halloween fairy tales. Satanic cults are bull dumbass. Anyway, we going anytime soon?" He pointed towards the living room where they could hear Vince playing his game.

"Ask him if he still has the shits. I left my jacket in Dana's room."

Jason reluctantly went to ask Vince if he was well enough to join them, while Adam entered his sister's room and grabbed the coat off her chair. He snooped through the term papers on her desk. Just essays on astronomy and one lengthy paper about mass riots in Quito Ecuador, way back in 1949. He didn't recognize the handwriting. His sister had a distinctive style and this was unfamiliar.

They'd drifted apart so much over the last several months. Dana didn't offer to help Adam with his costume this year though he hadn't planned on dressing up anyway. He was still hurt by the dismissal. The previous Halloween she'd made his deformed twin Belial out of papier-mâché and doll parts while he'd carried the monster around in a picnic basket. Their greatest costume collaboration ever.

He'd always been impressed by Dana's artistic skills and imagination, but she no longer watched cheesy Italian post-apocalyptic flicks with him and had lately taken to mocking his role-playing sleepovers and weekly trips to the comic book store.

Maybe she was right; maybe he was too old for superheroes and dungeon crawls and dressing up as his favorite movie monsters. He only had a fleeting connection with Vince and Jason these days, just habit that made him invite them over every other weekend to hang out. His mom seemed different lately as well. Even his dad had taken to spending most of his free time on his transistor radio hobby.

Adam wondered if Dana still drew cartoons or if she'd outgrown that too. He opened a drawer, moved around some loose sheets and pens, found a few unfinished drawings. One was more complete than the others, the charcoal and colored pencil applied so heavily he could feel the shading details. It was an illustration of the shed and woods behind their house with something that might be the rudimentary outline of a face scribbled across the tree line. Its bright blue eyes gleamed in stark contrast to the dark background.

He set it aside and found a sketch of an astronaut, hose trailing behind, the end drawn with jagged lines to show it had been severed. A thought balloon read *In space no one can hear me sing!!!*. Musical notes spread like ripples into a starry sky. The astronaut's nametag read **ADAM**.

Adam looked closer. They weren't music notes, but strange occult symbols. Whorls and spiky edged shapes coiled into shapes that hinted at pentagrams, threatened to coalesce into goat skull-shaped sigils.

He folded the cartoon and put it in his coat pocket.

When he joined Jason on the back porch he was disappointed to see that Vince was not there.

"No Vince?"

"Nope. Said he wanted to jerk off to Thundarr in private."

"Better than you spankin' it to Ookloa."

Adam glanced back at his house and wondered why his mom had placed a jack-o'-lantern on the porch when no trick-or-treaters had ever visited in all the years they'd lived here. He watched the pumpkin's candle flame grow smaller the deeper they traveled into the forest.

They continued walking into the woods while cracking crude jokes at each other's expense.

The rain fell in a fine layered mist. Adam was confused; they should've been on top of the Stanton house by now. He assumed if they cut across the mountain they'd come out near the murder house. So where was it?

He felt detached, floating above the trees, watching himself trudge along as the hill rose slightly. The area was covered in a lush carpet of moss that squelched at every step. The sweet scent of burning oak wafted from distant fireplaces. Jason kept swiping a thick branch against the trees, spraying chunks of bark with each blow. Adam winced at every strike; the thought of these centuries old woods being abused bothered him.

They reached the top of the rise. The trees thinned out below into a shallow valley darker than the drizzly night. A breeze dipped into the sunken area blowing an earthy odor into their faces, like moldering leaves or wet fur. The sky was obscured by plump black clouds. Adam thought there was a hint of illumination behind them.

"Jas', I think we must've walked by Stanton's house alre—".

Adam's flashlight illuminated a body partially buried by tangerine and scarlet veined leaves. He could make out an outline that suggested a petite head and legs roughly the size of a child's.

"Oh Jesus." Adam said. "I am so not going down there."

"What the hell wuss. Someone dumped their trash bags or something." Jason skidded down the short decline by pushing himself from tree trunk to tree trunk.

"See?" Jason tapped the form with his foot. It gave a hollow sound. Brushing the leaves away revealed a 3-foot tall Virgin Mary statue.

Adam moved forward for a better look. Something crumbled underfoot.

He moved his light to the object. It was a large plaster crucifix shattered into several powdery segments. The messiah's chest now bore a hole in the shape of his shoe.

Their flashlights reflected off of lacquered plaster fragments. Dozens of Christian icons were strewn about, the remnants of a few still hanging on the trees like folk art.

A branch cracked loudly somewhere in the woods.

"We're surrounded." Adam wasn't sure why he'd said it.

Jason assumed he was referring to the scattered figures, so he started to kick at the leaves to find more.

"Check this out." Jason held up another plaster Virgin Mary. She had a bright turquoise 5-pointed star glued to her neck. Her robe was spattered with red and black candle drippings.

Adam was both terrified and confident now that his faith in the spread of cults could no longer simply be dismissed as fundamentalist paranoia. "You know what this is. A coven. Gotta be. Halloween night. The murders. This desecration of Christ stuff." He looked around the forest nervously.

"Yeah, sure. A coven that worships things with pentagram faces. You might wanna grow some balls." Jason dropped the star-headed Mary and wiped his hands on his jeans. "Let's see what else is here."

They searched the forest floor and found a few more of the plaster human-headed Marys, but no more star-heads. Several of the ceramic crucifixes had been used for target practice. They hung crookedly from rusty nails in the trees, and judging by the pitted bark, a shotgun was involved at some point.

"You think the cops know about this?"

Jason snorted. "Probably just rednecks target shooting. Nothing illegal about that."

Adam persisted, emboldened by his fear. "What about star-faced Mary? Hillbilly arts and crafts? And tonight of all nights?"

"There's nothing against the law about arts. Or even crafts. We don't know when this happened so you can't blame Halloween. Some drunk inbreds were just shooting at Christian garage sale crap after running out of Rainier beer cans. You scared?" Jason was bored and wanted to head back.

Adam looked into the inky depths of the woods. The world was a shadow as far as he could see. An expanse of forest scents, the insinuation of hidden alcoves and dark glens waiting to be discovered.

"No. I'm not scared."

Jason tossed his branch into the foliage where it made a louder and lengthier than expected rustling.

"Good. Didn't wanna have to hold your hand on the way back. We'd better get going before Satanists take naked pics of Vince."

Vince floated in the cesspool of space.

Bobbed on foul currents past minor planets, chunks of

124

meteoroids, flotsam and jetsam sloshing in the black currents of infinity. The universe was a septic system. Stars floated in a murky flow only to be dumped down drains, flushed to earth where they gushed into a secret glade tucked away in the forest. Here a quiet presence wandered, its head a blue nimbus glowing like a bleeding star.

(Something awful will come through the window)

Vince woke up. He had fallen asleep on the couch with the TV still on. Pepto-Bismol churned in his stomach. He contemplated calling his mom to come pick him up. He was sticky with sweat, fever throbbed dully behind his eyes.

The voice must have been a combination of his dream and the TV. It sizzled like wet electricity in his memory. He usually remembered his nightmares, especially the recent Satan populated ones, but this one was elusive. Slippery like the wraiths in the deeper dungeon levels of his video game.

But why had he heard a voice?

The Intellivision was paused.

He heard someone talking again, a mumbling that popped like water splashed on hot grease.

But there were words in there, something coherent though he couldn't decipher the content. The sound seemed to be coming from the shed out back. He peered through the window. Were there trick-or-treaters out there? Adam had insisted nobody ever came this far into the boonies to beg for candy.

He jumped when something banged against the back door.

Adam and Jason were relieved to see the jack-o'-lantern on the porch steps. The boys were comforted by the sight of Vince at the window even if the flickering TV behind him cast a strange sapphire colored halo around his head and stretched his shadow further than it should. The back door was locked. Adam didn't remember locking it. He knocked loudly.

A few moments passed before Vince opened the door. "You losers scared the shit outta me. How'd it go?"

Jason threw his hands up. "Pointless. But we did find a buttload of statues shot all to hell."

"Really? Like bored hunters or something?"

"Probably. Though Adam thinks it was King Diamond." Jason laughed.

"Shut up ass-wad. The woods get pretty thick back there. Couldn't even find Stanton's house." Adam unzipped his coat and walked down the hall to the kitchen.

"Weird. Oh yeah, before I forget, why didn't you tell me your dad was coming by?" Vince asked.

"Because he's not. I already told you he's at work." Adam opened the fridge and grabbed a soda.

"There was someone out back. Thought it was trick-or-treaters but then I heard someone talking in the shed." Vince insisted.

"No you didn't. There's nobody else here. Just us two, plus one retard." Jason slurred his last few words in an exaggerated attempt to mimic someone with Down Syndrome.

"Way to be an asshole. I heard someone talking out there."

Adam set his soda down on the kitchen counter. "My dad works on his radios in there. Maybe he left one on."

"It did kinda sound like radio station interference."

"Mystery solved. Did you go check yet?" Jason pointed to the back door.

"It's cool. Adam's right. It was a radio."

"You didn't check? Hey, Vince is afraid of a ghetto blaster. Who here's not a pussy?"

"Don't be a dick Jas'," Adam said.

"He can't help being himself," Vince joked. "Hold on. Let me get my shoes."

The boombox in the shed was turned off. An electrical odor like soldered metal clung to the air but the various radio components and tools were still neatly arranged on the work table. There was no evidence of anyone having been there recently. Adam kept glancing towards the black rectangle of the shed's entrance.

"We done?" Jason asked.

"Weird. Don't know what you heard Vince. Had to be one of these radios." Adam reached into his jacket pocket and realized his sister's drawing was gone. He looked around the shed floor but it was nowhere in sight.

"What's up?" Vince asked.

"I lost something."

"What?" Vince sensed Adam was more worried than he let on.

"A drawing. You guys mind helping look for it? It's just a piece of paper with a cartoon on it."

His friends could tell it was important to Adam so they didn't ask any more questions. They walked back near the house to search within the porch light's radius. Adam knew he could've lost it anywhere between here and the graveyard of broken messiahs, but he sure as hell was not walking all the way back to that place by himself.

Adam moved away from the shed beyond its light source, watched Vince and Jason idly browse. His flashlight failed to pick up the glare of anything resembling a piece of paper. He walked a few more yards into the woods, looked back at his home. If the shadows moving in the kitchen were any indication Jason and Vince had already given up. "Jesus, guys. Sorry to take 3-minutes of your time." He mumbled to himself.

He was about to call it quits as well when he saw a blue light floating in the blackness. His first thought was of nature documentaries and the bulb at the end of some deep sea creature's tentacle.

Must be Jason screwing around with his lightsaber. Good ol' predictable Jason had decided to play another prank.

But the light wasn't in the elongated shape of a saber, it was more like a glowing ball the size of a fist. Maybe Jason had taken the plastic blade part off and was using the handle as a flashlight. Even so, Adam couldn't imagine how Jason had managed to get the light to float so high up in the air.

"Hey Jason!"

The orb jumped up and down like an agitated animal, then ascended as if whatever was holding it had scuttled up a tall tree. The profound depths of the woods made it difficult to gauge just how far away it was.

The blue light disappeared.

Adam remembered Jason had a red lightsaber.

He froze. A faint static crinkling sound like power lines in cold weather permeated the air.

"I'm heading back to my house moron!"

Something attempting to tread lightly through the leaves despite its bulk gave up any pretense of stealth and broke into a gallop. There was an uncomfortably long stretch between each tread— either Jason had impossibly lanky legs or he was covering a vast distance by hopping. A chittering sound flowed towards Adam like liquid pushed ahead of a massive underwater object.

Adam turned his flashlight off. His surroundings slowly congealed into focus. The house was just down the slope to his left, behind the enormous oak tree that blocked the porch light from illuminating much beyond the trunk. If he ran he could make it to the driveway in half a minute or less.

But he couldn't run as fast as he wanted. The branches whipped against his face and some were thick enough to do major damage. He slowed to a brisk walk and held his right forearm up to prevent any stray twigs from hitting him in the eyes.

Once he reached the outer edge of the porch light he'd formulated a plan to lock all the doors and keep Jason outside for an hour or more. Give him a taste of his own medicine.

A silhouette further down the hill moved from behind one tree to another.

"Screw you, Vince! This isn't funny!"

The figure peeked around the trunk. Vince must be wearing a tattered glow-in-the-dark Halloween mask that emitted a blue haze like the daikaiju's atomic breath on the black light poster thumb-tacked to his bedroom ceiling.

Someone had extinguished the candle in the jack-o'-lantern near the back door.

The kitchen window curtains parted slightly as someone walked by inside the house. Through the brief gap Adam saw Jason, head tilted back as if he were laughing at a joke. Probably his own.

Something shattered Adam's right arm.

The blow forced his ruined limb into his face. His forehead split from the impact of the jagged ulna. Bright azure stars filled his head.

Adam's limp body scraped across the ground away from the porch light deeper into the woods until whatever had pulled him away from the house released him. The only sound he could manage was a whimper. He tried to sit up but his body had a mind of its own.

A patch of sky opened. Unique constellations spun like coriolis deflected debris. *I'm going into shock. That must be why the stars don't look right.*

Adam saw bone poking through his jacket sleeve. Wet white and shining in the night air.

The buzzing sound increased, the woods submerged in a hum like the nervous crackle of insects in a disturbed nest. His head lolled over, the mossy ground cool against his cheek.

Adam saw Dana's folded drawing a few feet away. It was partially covered by a clump of moss. He began to cry.

His weeping turned hysterical when something enormous picked him up and spoke in a voice scoured by time,

Ready to play the Naked Movie Star game?

"You hear that?" Jason looked out the window but couldn't see anything beyond the black pane.

"What? Adam find his drawing?" Vince took a sip from his soda.

"Don't know." Jason walked to the back door, turned the hallway light off, cupped his hands against the window. "Whole lotta nothin' out there."

Adam stepped into view.

He was naked but still wearing shoes. The porch light glistened off of his skin. His neck hung at an odd angle. Leaves and dirt caked his face and chest.

"Holy shit," Vince gasped.

Jason frantically tried to open the door. Panic made him fumble. "Call an ambulance!"

Adam swayed in place, tried something that clumsily replicated a smile. A tinny tingle of a voice,

Trick-or-treat guys!

Vince grabbed Jason's arm, his face a stark exhibition of fear. "It's not Adam."

He couldn't fully explain why he was so certain Adam wasn't Adam *(Something awful)*, he couldn't use his dreams as evidence to convince himself much less Jason *(Through the window)*, but he knew he was right.

"What the hell Vince! Adam's hurt!" Jason looked around the kitchen for the cordless phone.

C'mon guys! We're gonna play the game now!

"It isn't him Jas'. Look at his mouth."

"Dammit Vince I—" Jason moved to shove Vince aside but

stopped when a young girl stepped out of the woods.

Her naked body had been repeatedly slashed, skin slathered with black blood from chin to shins. Both the girl's and Adam's mouths began to chatter. A blue glow frothed between their teeth.

"This isn't happening." Vince couldn't accept that Stanton's daughter was here, couldn't believe that this was the same Adam he'd known since kindergarten. He just wanted to be a child again when all he had to worry about was how late his parents would let him stay up.

Something moved in the woods. Ambiguous forms darker than the night sky shifted deep within. Vince was certain the encroaching wave of cobalt blue clouds was rearranging the position of the stars.

"Vince, I swear I'll kill you if this is some stupid payback prank." Jason backed away from the door.

"I must've picked up their interference in my sleep." When Jason looked at him with complete incomprehension, Vince whispered, "It's something worse than a conspiracy of Satanists."

The two boys pushed the dining room table against the door then threw the chairs on top for good measure. Jason saw the cordless phone on top of the microwave and grabbed it as they ran to Adam's bedroom for sanctuary. Inside, they wedged a chair under the door handle and pushed the bookshelf in front of the only window.

"The phone won't work." Jason's voice was high pitched and trembling.

In the chaos of barricading the room neither one heard the front door break or the rasp of the table sliding across the linoleum floor. They didn't hear footsteps stumbling down the hall like broken toddlers learning to walk.

The bedroom door shook.

"What are they?" Jason screamed.

Vince couldn't find the right words to explain how these intruders had prepared for their arrival by softening up the populace, making this world susceptible to cult hysteria. Couldn't describe how something had successfully plotted to disguise the arrival of the unfathomable.

The chair buckled, collapsed. The door flew open.

Stanton's daughter stood in the hallway behind Adam, flashes emitting from her mouth like the spark of wintergreen candy chewed in the dark. Adam stepped into the bedroom but his shadow was all wrong.

He moved incorrectly, like a bad movie special effect, the human eye catching the fact it wasn't Adam but a costume or mechanical puppet. Vince was grateful that whatever was actually responsible for inhabiting Adam remained out of sight, kindly sparing them an impression of its size.

"Oh Adam, oh no." Vince's voice was gentle, heartbroken, almost apologetic.

Jason's hands were shaking violently as if he were flicking water off his fingers. "Oh sweet Lord there it is. Their mouths are opening wrong. Oh God here it is." The collar of his Celtic Frost t-shirt was soaked from his crying.

"Oh Adam, oh—" and Vince never felt so alone or so sad in all his 13-years. He longed to believe that this was all just some human threat, that Halloween wasn't a liminal time for the realms of the unknown to bleed into the realms of the known. These things had been oh so clever in drawing attention away from their machinations by concocting Satanic panic hysteria.

Subterfuge for their inevitable visit.

The world tilted. An ocean colored shadow flowed to the corner of the room knocking the bookshelf on its side and exposing the window. A low bass vibration shook the air, the sound of deep time. A blue light sluiced through the clouds, an invitation for something ancient to crawl through the open sewers of the sky.

Adam spoke but the sound didn't match his mouth's movements.

Ready to play the Naked Movie Star game?

Jason started screaming as the urine stain on his pants spread.

The room was as cold as the vacuum of space. The thing failing at pretending to be Adam stared back at them with its cerulean gaze, the same color as the plaster of star-headed Mary's robes in the forest, a celestial hue that filled their heads with another's mind as Vince continued to plead *oh Adam, oh Adam, oh Adam* until their mouths and eyes and heads overflowed with that peculiar humming blue starlight and neither boy spoke with their own voice ever again.

SCARCELY HAVE THEY BEEN PLANTED

I ain't nothin' but dung clay sculpted by the Potter's Hand. Ain't nothin' but seed cultivated and done sown by the Lord. Been made not so smart on accounts a my bein' dumb so's I don't let worldly things corrupt. I'm grateful for this. I'm grateful for the Garden, even though the strangeness happens hereabouts.

Strange likes the time my aunty been only shortly dead when I seen her leaped out at the cool gray clays. Belly flopped 'cross the grass like a fat tadpole jumped from puddled mud. Sinked head first into what she'd called the "fertile loam".

That means the good dirt.

Right into them award winning melons patch. Aunty always fretted over those gourds.

Collette and Sammy helped poke about the garden, but we were without findin'. Collette opinionated that since aunty was no longer of this world, and the family done dirted her in the cemetery plot long befores, there ain't no good reason I seen her all naked and flopped about. So these days nobody regards my opinionating such 'cause I have the problems with bein' slow.

So I was waryin' that day when I was basketing plums. When I seen the stranger staring at the compost heap. Know she shouldn't be inside the fences.

She was going under and overs the mulch with her hands. To let steams out. Under and overs. Plums was too ripe and syrup so much the bees came flizzing like hot deerflies.

Don't like that.

The new lady was the prettiest I ever done seen. Hair colored like pennies at the bottom a the wishing pool when the sun is just so. Long like the house vines, but razored on one side. I was closer and seen she gots the scar-head, pushed in like a dented tin a blackberries. She was doing such a lovely song I was ashamed for the interruptin'.

Voice a birds. All like the choir sings the prettiest.

Her sounds brung the rememberin' of wakin' up in that compost long ago. I was a small girl way back. Dug outta the compost from bottoms on up. It done been a right ruckus. But I don't remember so good on account my skull is thin. Likes loose snake skin.

Under and overs.

This ain't really ever been happened. I mean my head *is* slight, that's not for arguin', but sleepin' beneaths rotten egg skins? Mold leaves and browned lettuce?

I just don't.

My past is hazy as the fogged garden in the morn'. I seen giant shapes move about real slow out there. They was brayin' like big donkeys. I was not knowin' what the shapes was.

This lady pawin' at the compost right befores me was like that—I know she's there, but not the why. All that confusion done got me the déjà vu that brings the sick.

"I'm Jolene." I said by way of introducing.

"My name is Annabelle." She said. Her face and hands was filthing.

"Hi Annabelle, my belle." I hepped her away from the fertilizer puffin' up warm in the damp. I was blushed in bein' sorry.

She smelled like wet dirt. Things gone bad. Earthworm perfume.

Annabelle's ways was kind but strangely, like that three-legged kitten I leaved a bowl of cream 'til the 'coons or opossums done to her. I reckon Annabelle was what I hear folks calls an anomaly.

That's a kind way a sayin' they is slow in the noggin.

But I was such too on not being smart enough to live like people in the nicest houses, but not dumb enough to live in one of them homes for disabled folks. I works real hard for gramma.

Annabelle pinched on my cheek. She had poop fingers. I didn't want to hurt no feelings so I smiles real big, but not so I shows all my mouth and scare her.

"You're why I believe in God." Annabelle said. Oh my but the Lord gone and blessed her with a voice that made my guts feels like the colorin' of wild strawberries in spring.

"God don't make no junk." I didn't know what that meant, but heard it so many times I had to speech my airs.

"Most of what God makes is junk. That's why you're such a joy." That voice a hers. Like the sweet alyssum bloom in my ears.

I asked if it be gramma takin' her in, or if she found our home by accidents, or her moms or pops dropped her hereabouts. But she was empty with conversating.

Garden be such a big place it took me and Annabelle a ways in travelin'. Area bigger than ten houses stacked together like wood-piled. Sammy told me so I believes, and he is being truthful. He's like a brother. I don't know who his moms and pops is.

Takes up so much land we walks damn near an hour. From here to there and back again is the works. There's plenty a planter boxes. So many fruit trees you get lost playin' and seekin'. Leafy greens and bulbs of such colors and sizes I don't even know. A veritable cornucopia, gramma says as is her way.

We follow the big fence that circled high as the trees, higher than two of me and maybe one Sammy on shoulder-top almost falling for topples. Fence was sticked with barbed wire. Bent at the top. Leaned inside the garden so as to keep deers from the jump over.

Sure would keep the talls from hopping out too.

Sammy was out in the garden somewhere. Annabelle and me never seen him. That region is so full a exalted spaces he could a been anywhere.

We got home and Annabelle washed up real nice. Swished my face watery too.

Gramma was makin' supper. Good kind a supper of burnt skins and hot applesauce and blackened onions. Collette was kitchen helpin'. She weren't inclined much to do in the ways of conversating.

"Look what I found in the garden!" I was shined as a peacock. Like I found my very own friend and we was goin' to a movie or a dance. Annabelle's beauty made me feel the ways I do when I hear gramma chanting. Or the smells from the garden in the time of blossoms.

"Ah yes. Sweet Annabelle. She has come to stay. Jolene dear. Would you be so kind as to show her around?"

Most reckon gramma's voice would be frogged, but mine has a lady lilt. Smooth as fish eggs. I liked when she'd get to weavin' her stories from her books. Didn't understand half, didn't believe the other half, but the speaked ones were telled real good.

That's all that mattered.

Gramma is like the river when rains brim and gets to sputter with mad dog foams. Old but strong. And you'd better listen or she'll show you things and a thing or two. Her hands is the loveliest. Put 'em in a brass cage and they'd sing.

She done laid those hands on my face once. I had visions a the orchard. Thick fruits and strange vegetables when the garden was first growed in the dreamin'. The plot a land came to be so long ago I ain't got words for it. Gramma says no soul been able to invent any such words.

I showed Annabelle 'round the property.

Inside our home the shelves is dipped with canned jars. Lids wear dust crowns so the foods inside might not be wholesome.

Some is for hearty foods.

Some is for gramma's concoctions.

Some is with blobs that look like something I found in a chicken egg. Annabelle kept up with the touchin' a gramma's jars and bottles and such. All curious with the wonders.

I tells Annabelle that gramma raised those with nothing to their name but the clothes on the back and a prayer. I never seen no prayers, though gramma and Sammy and Collette make their hands together when praying like they is holding wet tadpoles between their palms.

I don't know about this. Never seen nothing in them hands no matter how prayerful I gets, or how long they be holdin' like that.

I tell Annabelle about the two staircases in the room you walk into. Through the door at the front. One steps goes to the bedrooms. I don't know where the other steps goes.

This is off limits.

That's when Collette showed. Standin' at the tops a them stairs as if she be knowin' we was on the walk. Scolds us to not even dare think a goin' up them off limit stairs.

She is an angel of vengeance. Hair fire bright. Dress the color a wet pomegranates. Sewed it together her own self. She done tried to teach me of the sewin' but I ain't got the knack. Collette's voice got the teeth inside.

"Jolene, you know better."

I'm afraid 'cause she's lit with ornery.

"Sorry Collette. I am." I said as my ways is when all ain't so clear as to the why's and the what's.

Collette gave me stab-eyes.

I held Annabelle's hand as gentle as if I was dustin' one a gramma's old porcelain knickknacks. We left soft, like steppin' between rows of cabbages.

Outside I tells Annabelle the apple green butterflies is my best. I seen no wild rabbits out there in the garden for a spell. There is birds. I like birds lots but they sing real scratchy these days, like Sammy's rusty chainsaw when he chops up the trees knocked down in the storm. He cuts them the way gramma cuts my sausages on my plate for supper I like the best.

Annabelle said she got done with in the head when a hay truck slipped the brake. Rolled down a hill overs her. Didn't know so good after that. But I ain't of much when it comes to such matters. Family couldn't look after her no more, as the money to pay the doctors up and went. So she comes here. I let her know it's a good place and a good family and we're happy.

We conversated about people who says you can see the stars on the day if you look up from the bottom of a chimney. I done tried this in the empty well, but it ain't ever worked.

But it do work in the garden.

When I stand in the center next to the compost pile, and looks at the sky when the sun be out, I can see all the stars that ever was. Bright as fireflies. Don't think it ever ends none either.

Annabelle took to hummin' that same tune she'd been on when I first seen her at the compost. Sound like warm syrup and rose hips.

I thinked it might be nice to tell her of the truth on how my mama had the growths on the innards. So I tells Annabelle how when I was but a small girl my mama took me outside to see a lunar eclipse. That's when the moon goes hiding from the Earth's shadows.

I looked up. All that stuff going on with no stoppin' at the Heavens made me dizzy. There was so much room between each light I was filled with the spirits. Oh how I was tremblin' to get lost in them black empty fields. Mama called them patches the Illimitable Garden.

Mama told to me gather rocks from around the flower bed. Cuffed my jeans and put the rocks in there so I wouldn't fall up and get lost for all a time.

Felt them stones tuggin' at my legs. Saved me from jauntin' to Heaven as a dandelion seed at hurricane time. Me and mama watched that lunar eclipse and I wasn't afraid.

When mama went to dirts I felt like I did with no rocks in my jeans. I miss her. Gramma says we'll be together at the next bumper crop. I think that means not so long a waitin'.

Annabelle seemed of a dubious mind when I be finished with my mama story.

I took Annabelle strollin' between rows of corns, leaves shaped like tips a spears I seen in serial jungle adventures they show at the pictures for three dimes. Annabelle took up her tune again when we passed by the wasp nest. Makes me feel sick with the runs when I looks at it too long. It was a queer nest.

It winked at me once.

Sometimes it's laughin' and times it's not. But that could a been the wasps flyin' around it angry and clickin'. Clickin' like that electric fence I dropped the dead snake on when I ain't knowed no better. Sammy said I should a learned of the ways when I done squat-pissed on the fence up from the tree branch that one time.

But I'm not learned quite right as I mentioned before.

Annabelle stopped hummin' her music after we'd strolled the garden a piece. Over the days she got real nervous about that region. Started to stay away. Stopped taking walks altogether.

I was still pleased to gift Annabelle flowers from the garden, but she was feelin' right terrible for that space. I never understood why. All that grows has its place on God's green and red Earth. Why fret over the seed and the bloom?

One time she wept tearful when I gifted hibiscus pink as baby field mice. Said they growed in obscene circumstances. But nothin' so beautiful could ever be called obscene.

137

It's likely I was not of full understandin'.

Annabelle began to poke the house and property on her own. Peekin' and findin'. Gone "exploring" she said and did. I never done this for it ain't proper for a lady to do. Ain't sure why, but I remember something uncouth about such.

I know my parents must a been disappointed birthin' a daughter so stupid she gots no reason to be. They was in the rights in leaving me with gramma. Maybe I don't deserve a buryin' in the compost heap. All this hatin' myself I couldn't even cry because I deserves nothin'.

Worthless.

I been called a dummy so much I know I outlived my welcome on this planet.

But Annabelle made me happy. I was feelin' funny at how happy she made me. I wanted her to be full a glad too, to stop turnin' over and stop eyeballin' secret places and stop questionin'. I was heartached with concern.

So it all come to be the way it is when Annabelle came callin' late one night. After I done dipped the hot bath and dressed for pillows. Tapped real light on my door. I was wearin' pajamas. My heart was fit to lift on her visitin' me in such a ways.

She squeezed my hand too tight, said, "I want you to leave with me. We cannot speak."

I did as was her wants. Weren't wearin' no shoes.

She took me on the off limits stairs, of which I was never knowin' where they went and was never supposed. I was not enjoyin' our stroll this time.

We made cat-paws past chestnut bookshelves with slag glass bric-a-brac. Tin plaques of the auctions and feed stores and other places I'd only fancied ever goin'. Rows a gramma's ruckus books. All done up in leather skins. Strange writin' on the sides that made me taste the tingly of toothed pennies.

Went through a hall of peeled wallpapers pretty with the hoof-horse carousels. I had the same in my room when I was a little girl.

Tippy-toed past a laundry area. Piles a clothes all tored up like some poor soul been stuck by the barb wire. The only sound came from our feet on floorboards squeakin' like rats scritchin' wallboard.

"Ain't allowed here Annabelle my belle."

Annabelle placed her palm against my mouth. Shook her head so serious I was of the fear she was gettin' to scold. Her hand skin smelled of wild lavender.

We kept the hallway a going. It rigged to the side. Ended at a mahogany door. Base all scuffed as if a wild mutt done penned here hungered fierce. Annabelle tugged my hand. Makin' me go to shadows on the knees.

Pointed into the room.

My family sat at a dinner table. They was holdin' hands in silent prayer. This is the best kind for worship.

Candle on the wooden table lit up lows the color a butter. Couldn't make heads but could see the torn up cuffs a Collette's red blouse. Big shape a Sammy. Gramma's youthful hands.

It was a banquet. Pink ham and dark roast beef with roasted potatoes. Golden rolls. Bright green collards. Their plates was piled with somethin' I couldn't see. My stomach hollered. Annabelle gave me a look. My family didn't move not a muscle.

I slid on my rump away. Low-voiced said this was a child's game. Ain't playin' no more. Annabelle grabbed my hand. I stopped movin'. What did that girl want of me?

Gramma started the swayin' as she was in a religious way and a reverend was hootin' out the demons. Collette and Sammy did likewise after a spell.

Gramma, then Sammy, then Collette stopped the religious back and forth. Stopped then start shovelin' food stuffs off a plates with hands a pale grubby fingers that looked like fat tree roots. Ate like they was starved.

Clumps fell on the floor. My family ignored the feast on the table, all satisfying and hot, just ate the platefuls heaped up. Fingers made an awful racket on them plates like twigs scratchin' at glass.

Annabelle whispered that she sure hoped they wouldn't bob their heads low enough to see faces.

This was silly. This was my family and there weren't a thing to fear. But it sure started to stink awful. I scooted to see what'd spilled from the plates.

My family was eatin' composts from the garden.

Annabelle looked at me kind a sad, kind a scared. Full a wonderin' with wide animal eyes.

I remembered. Memory pot done got all stirred up.

I telled Annabelle a story. A story about that time my family and me done picked clays from the river's banks and mucked it with composts to shape into somethin' that reminded us of what my mama used to look like.

Annabelle got all saucer-eyed. Begged me to whisper.

But I kept up with talkin'. Told her how we all collected as many stingin' insects as our mason jars would hold. Collette was bestest at this. Wasps, hornets, bees, mosquitoes, centipedes–you names it. Them bugs jumbled like they was tryin' to break outta glass prison.

Put the jars mouth down over mulch-mama's brain, her heart, where her private lady parts would a been.

The bugs stung and bit. All that venom juice oozed. Sank deep into mama's soft soil body with all a life's ichor. Oh how I remembers gramma singin' such a ruckus as to make my heart ache with hope.

Annabelle's sobbin' and beggin' me to shut up was so as to make me hatin' my own self even more. But I went on with the tale.

Mama didn't flower. Only lasted long enough to hold my hand for a moment's time. Gramma's works or not, it don't do that way. When one a God's children be returned to the lush humus they transform just like the spirit's seed on a floatin' to the Heavens.

Mama took to dirts once more.

Gramma must a heard me tellin' tales, or maybe it was Annabelle's sad wailin' that got to her—whichever it be, her head nodded like after too much wine. Face got closer to the buttery candle light. Seen her skin grayed and papery as them wrinkly walls of a wasp nest. Opened her mouth but all that come out was a puff a wasps all flizzin'.

Annabelle screamed and screamed.

'Fore I could blink she done ran down the hall. Clopped down them stairs 'til I heard the front door slam, then footsteps on the gravel driveway.

Was fit to be done I was.

I'd been treated with chemicals that made it so I couldn't feel adult things, like the sexy stuff or makin' the babies. On account of my low cunning as it was for the best. But I was heartached for Annabelle.

I ain't knowin' if I was in love, 'cause I can't feel like that no more, but bein' near Annabelle made me wild with pride and scared I was fillin' up my soul so much. Took to slappin' my face real hard like I did when I was a little girl. To make the thoughts jostle away to the empty spaces between the stars.

I'm stupid, but not so dumb I believe Annabelle had love for me.

But I could pretend.

Kinda like I do when I dream a papa drivin' up in his truck and he says he made a mistake and he was so sorry he and mama dropped me off at gramma's to live and maybe we could go fishin' and I could move in with him. Wouldn't that be nice?

I imaginate these ways that sometimes help me feel less sad. I can't decide such for I should a been left to rot at birth.

Gramma and Sammy and Collette rose up from their dinner table all slow and patient like they was decidin' who'd be clearin' the table. They walked right past me, didn't even look at me, walked down the hall to the steps. I heard the front door open and close again. I heard a commotion comin' from the garden.

Annabelle took to screamin' right 'bout then.

I ran out the front door, across the lawn to the garden where the heavens was full a fog and mists a roots come down from what be up there and what is bein' on the ground.

Gramma and Collette stood around the compost pile. Their faces was fuzzy from the compost steamin' hot and moists like wet animals. Didn't have a notion where Annabelle be at.

Sammy was last into the garden. Ducked real lows under the fence for having growed even taller. My family moved around the compost, hand holdin', with their queer ways a walkin' and singin'.

And their new heads. Like thistledown on the wind.

I heard what sound like that old familiar tune, but that can't be 'cause I don't see Annabelle nowhere. But her voice be comin' from under the ground, like song through dirt clod mouth. That honey-sweet song filled me with joy 'cause I remembered them words, just likes the way mama chanted them in the days of the past:

Scarcely have they been planted,
Scarcely have they been sown,
Scarcely has their stock taken root in the earth,
But She merely blows on them, and they wither,

And the storm carries them away like stubble.

I hope Annabelle is ok. She must a gone a wiltin' on some distant soil. I admit I was jealous regardin' what a ruckus she be seein'. I know she be visitin' soon enough.

Hope mama likes her.

Looks to be the good kind a harvest. Sometimes it's hours a waitin' for the blossoms to be all smiles.

The Illimitable Garden is all aflutter tonight.

INTAGLIOS

Sunstone was going to burst out of the sand on his motorcycle any moment now. Revenant come from Hell. Breath stinking of meth-rot, phosphorescent eyes glowing brighter than the ghost orbs of Oriflamme Canyon.

Straight out of the ground. Like the biker gang leader from *Psychomania*. That film scared Amy shitless when she was six.

But Sunstone and his teen bride Phoenix were miles away. Squatting in their beat up orange van. Dead motorcycle tied down to the roof.

Sunstone and *Phoenix*. Bad ass biker names. A smidge of hippy clinging to them, like the stink of patchouli oil.

Far from here.

Nobody was after her.

Except for that mysterious figure trailing behind. Always keeping their distance. A half-mile or so back.

Just some hitchhiker bringing up the rear. Antsy Amy shouldn't have taken all those black beauties.

Sand stirred a few feet to her right. A lizard scurried across her foot.

Easy there Godzilla, she said.

Moonlight brushed the sagebrush fields, a vast carpet of straw colored foliage with traces of vibrant green in the younger ones. Amy's backpack was heavy, her feet aching and raw, sunburnt shoulders peeling to expose fresh skin. The desert sun had scorched away that new growth as well.

I'm a fucking walking matryoshka doll. She said to a large bush that shuddered in response.

Hopefully just another lizard.

Layers beneath layers.

She found it liberating to be under the desert sky with nothing weighing her down except a backpack. She was glad she'd decided to travel from Eureka to San Diego on foot-knew the area like the back of her hand, loved the desert regions most of all. Lived for the nothingness broken up by the occasional Joshua tree.

But that person back there. What were the odds another hitchhiker would be out and about at this early hour? Nobody stopped to pick people up off the highway anymore.

And she kept hearing weird shit. Voices that didn't belong in the desert.

She'd no moral qualms about partying with Sunstone and Phoenix earlier—they'd provided the free dabs and beer, when all she'd had on her was a teener. Not a fair trade, but they'd been accommodating.

Not likely to be Sunstone or Phoenix following. Amy couldn't imagine either of them being up for trekking across the desert. And what would be the point when they had their orange van?

Nobody had driven by in awhile. She felt like the last person alive on the planet.

Someone began speaking again.

Rumbling voice, occupying more of the air than she thought possible for something not pressed directly against her ear. She couldn't make out the words.

She'd heard something similar before, off the 15, past the town of Kelso, over the rolling dunes decorated with sporadic patches of scraggly dried grasses, deep into Death Valley. The vibration of shifting grains of sand had created a booming, brass instrument-like resonance. A weird geological phenomenon. She'd felt the sound in her torso.

Must be something seismic going on her as well. It just sounded like a person talking.

Or maybe radio waves. Transmission bouncing from satellites. Off the surface of planets.

Weird atmospherics picking up stuff.

What had Sunstone gone on about?

Unexplained shit in the desert.

Secret government projects, experiments instigating urban warfare, reverse engineering alien technology, Black Ops maneuvers, holes to the center of the planet.

Social manipulation.

Sunstone insisted the government faked the moon landing in Death Valley. Filmed the pick-ups on a secret Warner Bros backlot.

Mars Curiosity and Spirit rover footage was fabricated in Red Rock Canyon, but not so convincingly the conspiratorially adept hadn't found a lizard in a shot, miner's helmet in another.

Even one pic of a woman sitting on a rock.

Paranoid rants. Amy had to give the hippy fucks credit for their tenacity. Especially Phoenix who'd been adamant about the conspiracy.

You do know that Mars is landfill now? You follow? Incinerator plants up there disguised as pyramids. Trash, cars, all kinds a waste dumped on the surface. Even advertising statues poking out of the Martian soil. Follow?

At the time Amy had been amused that the conjecture was based solely on the couple's ignorance of paredolia.

But she'd listened politely, staring at the pale grit stuck to the grease between the folds on Sunstone's wrinkled forehead. He'd looked like an old-timey borax miner straight out of the Boron Mine. Face made harsh and haunted by desert living.

Phoenix reminded Amy of an illustration of *La Llorona* she'd glimpsed between the pages of a kid's ghost book long ago. Ratty white nightgown covered with stains. Long black hair, so straight and lustrous you could run fingers through it uninterrupted.

And her eyes.

She could've sworn they'd been all pupil, shimmering like motor oil when she was near the firelight, so it always looked as if she were on the verge of tears.

Amy had encountered their type plenty of times on her adventures; desert rats were all over the small ghost towns throughout California. At least these two hadn't been L.A. weekend tourists flocking out here to ride three-wheelers across the landscape, tearing up the ground, disturbing the flora and fauna. Just a burnout hippy and his teenage fuck toy.

Amy imagined Charles Manson's kids growing up to be like these two desert dwellers—though Sunstone had to have been too old, and

Phoenix too young. She didn't know for sure. She was no expert on Manson genealogy.

Then Sunstone had gone and confirmed Amy's suspicions:

Free of the Jew here in the desert. And Black agitators.

He'd expounded on his racist philosophy, an ideology that was more a clusterfuck of 18th century pseudo-anthropology and paranoid conspiracy theories than anything remotely coherent.

Some races are the degenerate offspring of orangutans. Some the wicked progeny of chimpanzees and gorillas.

Phoenix had been over the moon at having a new pair of ears to explain how she and Sunstone had dropped off the grid a few years ago, to live in a deep hole in the desert. Let the race wars thin the herds. Pop back up beneath skies raining flakes of blood and winds blowing wet blood and they'd cleanse themselves in oceans of coagulated blood when the world was reborn with pristine blood red skies.

Amy thought that was a whole helluva lot of blood.

After the End comes we'll wake up on another planet. Probably Mars. Only be white people living on the red planet. We'll ride out to rescue the orphaned white babies left behind. We'll be their saviors.

Reborn on that new planet.

Rebirth.

Repopulate.

Hadn't the Manson clan also gone on about digging a hole so deep in the desert they'd hunker miles beneath the surface? Cut a big ol' slit into the ground, crawl down with the huddled mass of idiot cowards waiting out the End of Times they so fearfully, and joyously, anticipated. Fuck and snack on acid, sleep it off 'til Armageddon rolls on by like a Rocky Mountain Double hauling hellfire.

Amy found it all too familiar.

She'd wanted to tell the racist fanatics to fuck off a few times. But she held back. She had a canister of pepper spray in one pocket, and a Blue Belt in Krav Maga in her muscle memory—she'd been confident she could take the wrinkly old scrotum sac and his bitch. Nothing to worry about here. Desert junkie trash. Partied with worse.

Goddamn Manson groupies. Sorry junkies probably squatted at Spahn Ranch and Barker Ranch at some point in their lives.

She'd attempted to placate the hostile mood by making a joke about whites, her own red hair, and Neanderthal genetics.

Descended from cavemen. Ha ha.

This hadn't gone over too well.

Amy didn't know why she was a weird magnet. How she'd managed to stumble across Sunstone and Phoenix in the middle of nowhere, huddled around a campfire beside their orange van, well, this was another of life's mysteries. Maybe it had something to do with her folk's brush with the Manson cult. That decades old incident had left a residual curse on her. The tale was firmly entrenched in her family's lore.

It was '69, her parents newlyweds spending a second night in their new home. Her dad woke up to the screen door tapping shut. He'd grabbed his shotgun and crept to the back of the house just in time to see two people slip over the fence down into the wash. Stepped back inside to realize the couch had been moved, and silverware scattered on the dining room table. He'd gone into the kitchen to call the cops.

Someone had taken a dump on the linoleum floor.

Years later her parents read about the Manson Family's creepy-crawling expeditions. The Family shit on floors, moved furniture, wrote spooky poems on the walls.

All to create an environment of fear.

Amy had known her conversation with Sunstone and Phoenix wasn't going to improve, so she'd thanked them for the high, then hightailed it out of there. They just watched her as she walked away. Sunstone's weathered face set hard like dried clay, while something wistful touched Phoenix's expression.

Amy noticed the figure following her about half an hour after she'd left the camp.

Something wasn't right about any of this.

Few hitchhiked these days. FBI propaganda in the 60s had scared off a large percentage of hitchhikers. By the late 70s it had dramatically decreased in popularity.

Amy was well aware that she was more likely to be raped or killed by someone she knew than some random stranger giving her a lift. Didn't accept many ride offers anyway; preferred to enjoy the scenery on foot.

No reason to stop now.

Seen a lot of things in California. Hiked to the Devil's Postpile in

Mammoth with a bunch of German tourists. Hoofed it over desert regions where rumors of one, if not several, MGM lions had met their final resting place. Explored the Tierra Blanca Mountains for any evidence that a long rumored Viking ship was buried there. No luck finding it.

Visited the Blythe Intaglios just off the 95. Ancient Quechan had removed the dark rocks on top of the ground to expose the lighter colored earth, creating petroglyphs of giant people. A few animals too.

That was a transcendent experience.

Mountain air flowed from the North, down into the desert, mingled with the hot and dry. Amy was cold but sweating. The night glinted with a blue sharpness. Numbed cheeks and chapped lips.

Rebirth. Repopulate.

It's-a cold and-a dry out here! she shouted, intentionally misquoting her favorite movie to take her mind off the memory of Phoenix's speech. That's right, a lovely stroll in the desert. Tra-la-la, isn't this fun?

Her outburst made her feel a bit better.

She glanced over her shoulder. The figure was still there.

No werewolves in these here parts.

Chupacabra maybe.

I'm a goddamn weird magnet.

Maybe there was a supernatural force that drew her to locations the Manson Family had lived, where his sycophants gathered, polluted the soil with their misdeeds.

Mapped out ley lines in blood and sand.

That's just crazy talk.

She wasn't some conspiracy nut like Sunstone and Phoenix, but she had a different way of looking at things. She wasn't convinced that Manson ever commanded anyone to kill. Everything pointed to that psychopath Tex. The prosecutor had concocted a tall tale to paint Charlie in the worst possible light.

A witch-hunt.

Portray hippies, flower children and revolutionaries as social movements that threatened the status quo, as a violent threat. Same went for the propaganda about hitchhiking—the government had taken something innocuous, launched a campaign to vilify it, then

148

scared people into acquiescing to authority.

All about perspective.

Like the giant intaglios she'd seen in Blythe. Have to be up in the air to fully appreciate what'd been created. Same for the Nazca lines in Peru—the immensity of their presence could only be understood from high above. They were even visible from space.

Scratch the surface and all kinds of new faces will greet you.

The hitchhiker had closed the gap.

Amy looked at her phone. There were no bars. Another patch of desert dead zone. It was 4:48 a.m.

A voice crackled in her ear:

WUR NEE REENG MRRS!

LANDYS ISS IMM NANT!

She frantically looked around. Sound carried far in the desert. Had to be a blaring radio miles away. It spoke again, more clearly:

WE ARE NEARING MARS!

LANDING IS IMMINENT!

It just happened to sound like Sunstone's voice. This bothered Amy on a level she couldn't fully rationalize.

Mars.

Some regions of the desert *did* look like Mars' surface, craggy and pitted and cinnamon red. Aztec Sandstone outcrops, nearly 200 million years old, suffused with vibrant shades of vermillion. Sunstone had certainly thought Red Rock Canyon looked like the fourth planet from the sun.

The figure had gained on her. Amy walked faster.

This is so fucked up.

Mars.

I'm walking on another planet.

She was spooking herself. Between the racist hippies and the weird radio broadcast and this hitchhiker, she was all nerves. At this pace Amy estimated they'd catch up in 15-minutes or less. It was past time to take evasive action.

She cut off the main highway along a shallow path that ran into the desert. Set her backpack on the ground, kneeled behind a clump of scrub brush.

It didn't take long. The figure arrived, trotting at a fairly good pace. Stick thin legs looked barely substantial enough to sustain their weight. Amy tried to make herself smaller, to blend into her surroundings. She peeked between the branches of sagebrush.

It was Phoenix.

Why is she after me?

She inhaled a breath in preparation to call out.

Then paused.

Phoenix was nude. Her bare skin slick with a cottage cheese-like substance.

Like a newborn covered in vernix.

Rebirth.

Amy crouched back down.

Where was Sunstone? Why wasn't he pulling up in that filthy orange van of his? She hadn't seen any vehicles for a suspiciously long time. It was early, but truckers used this route and some should've driven past by now.

Phoenix continued up the highway.

Amy waited until she was certain she was far ahead. Only then did she sling her backpack on, kept low, walked as close to the tops of the scrub brush as she could to avoid silhouetting herself against the waxing crescent moon. It was difficult what with the backpack's weight and her weariness, but she managed to keep Phoenix in sight.

She walked parallel with the road, about 40-feet into the desert, a mottled hill of dark boulders to her right. She was ready to drop on a dime if Phoenix turned to look back.

Repopulate.

A hill moved.

Amy let out a surprised cry, immediately clamped her hands over her mouth.

A few weeks ago she'd visited the Ubehebe volcanic crater, cut across the Teakettle Junction to the Racetrack Playa—a dry lake bed surrounding a rock monolith called The Grandstand. The tan-colored clay looked like an alien planet's surface. Here she'd seen the traveling rocks.

Of course she hadn't caught anything in the act; the rocks slid at a glacial speed, probably due to the lakebed freezing, winds nudging them along imperceptibly over time. The stones had left smooth depressions in the cracked surface, like slug trails.

But rock formations this large couldn't do that. Hills and

mountains didn't move.

Her exhaustion wasn't helping oxygen reach her brain efficiently. She'd breathed in some nasty desert varnish infected with spores, now multiplying in her lungs, spreading through her bloodstream, invading her brain.

Oh shit, maybe I have Valley fever.

But she felt fine. Her aches and pains were perfectly normal. No cough, no fever. Just traces of the drugs and the desert playing with her head.

I'm not that woman in the Mars Rover photo.

Now why would that even occur to her?

She continued walking.

A nimbus of light softened the horizon. The land became clearer, more distinct against the backdrop of a violet dawn. The world clotted into a tangible image, as if God had scratched away a stratum of dark gravel to reveal lighter soil underneath. An intaglio etched into existence by an unseen hand.

A towering bird-headed humanoid towered before Amy.

An RV-sized rooster stood at its side.

Several giant sentries looked out over the desert.

Amy's first instinct was to run, but the titans didn't reach out for her. Didn't move at all.

Phoenix's shape slipped into the shadows cast by the huge figures.

Amy almost called out to her but hesitated. She tentatively approached.

A 30-foot tall astronaut greeted her. He was holding a silver rocket ship in his large hands. She recognized him as the famous Gemini Man.

Fiberglass statues. Her relieved voice carried softly in the air. Shouldn't you be on display back east?

He didn't respond.

More like Mars Man.

She immediately regretted the thought.

Maybe this was an abandoned carnival. Or theme park. Something like the old L.A. Zoo hidden away in the hills. But why had Phoenix come here of all places? Without a stitch of clothing?

And what was she covered with?

Goddamn hippies and their weird ass sex games.

Amy walked past the Gemini Man. This wasn't an amusement park, but an expanse of broken down vehicles. A graveyard of scrap metal and deserted advertising statues.

Roadside Muffler Men.

Colossal fiberglass things, most built in Venice in the 60s to be used as advertising icons.

Must be a dump to dispose of them. Or a place where they did repairs.

Bird-head held a bucket of chicken out, offering a meal to weary travelers. A Uniroyal Gal that looked to have been altered into a waitress for some long closed diner stood vigil. Another giant held his arms frozen in position, as if the lost muffler would appear in his hands if he just waited everything out. The 15-foot tall rooster's body was a dingy white, its comb still bright red. A leg had been snapped off, the stump balanced on a rusted engine block.

Amy had seen junkyards out here in the desert before, but nothing on this scale. Strange how the place wasn't even surrounded by a security fence.

Hello? Bronson? I brought a case of Tenafly Viper.

She was pretty sure the place had no rent-a-cops on duty, and even more certain that, even if there were, nobody would get her joke.

There wasn't any outdoor lighting, though the moon was bright enough to maneuver between the mounds of metal.

A wasteland of American cars and trucks from different eras surrounded her. She touched the hood of what looked to be the remnants of a Plymouth Roadrunner. Kicked the tire of a crushed Pontiac Chieftain.

Rows of broken down cars and parts collected in disorderly stacks as far as Amy could see. A graveyard of rust and broken plastic, windshields cracked into spider web displays, shredded tires, warped grilles.

Real Route 66 Americana shit.

She was turned around, no longer sure if the highway was at her back or in front of her.

Something moved within the junkyard.

Amy focused between a tunnel of twisted vintage automobiles. She wondered why some looked less like cars and more like the remains of planetary rovers.

On the other side, through the opening, a light turned on inside an orange van.

The night filled with the roar of metal and glass crashing down in an avalanche of debris. A massive Indian's face suddenly filled the gap, his feather headdress a stereotypical anachronism.

Something had given. The precariously stacked automobiles had collapsed, started an avalanche of parts that tipped the fiberglass Indian over. The clatter of glass and metal was the junkslide subsiding, not the racket from one of the Muffler Men running away.

What the fuck else could it be?

Amy's field of vision was limited by the Indian head. She peered around the obstruction, through the diminished crack. She could still see the side of the van. A sliver of dusty orange.

The vehicle's door slid open. Dislodged a thin shape.

Phoenix? Amy said with little conviction in her voice.

Another form exited the van.

Then another.

A steady progression of shadows spread out into the junkyard.

They were still on the other side of the wreckage, and Amy used to run track in high school—all she had to do was sprint between the trash heap on the left, straight shot to the desert, to the road beyond. Run until a car came by.

If a car drove by.

Every cab light inside all of the dead vehicles turned on.

Amy wasn't sure which way to go. *Was it left then another left?*

She was discombobulated, but wasn't about to panic like some hysterical woman in a shitty horror film.

Fuck it. Change of plan. Monkey up the mountain of cars. Drop down on the other side.

The growl of thousands of engines turning over echoed amongst the piles of scrap.

She clambered over the auto graveyard. The passengers beneath her violently thrashed about in their seats as they eagerly reached out. The mountain of metal shook.

Amy slipped, flailed in an attempt to find something to grab onto, slid down the smooth humps of vintage vehicles.

Her leg snagged on something jagged. She fell to the ground on her side, the wind knocked out of her. The protrusion of fender that had sliced her skin wide open wobbled as if drawing attention to its culpability. A flap of knee lay against her shin.

She struggled to climb back up. Blood made the surfaces slick and difficult to maintain a grip.

I don't wanna be reborn.

Amy didn't know why the thought wouldn't leave her alone.

She incrementally inched her way higher. She was calmed by the lack of any light pollution, the early morning sky so perfect and clean it was like looking at the inside of a polished bowl flecked with pinpoints of light. Something liquid about all of it, as if space was an inverted ocean and only the weird actions of gravity kept the cosmic fountains from drowning this world.

She was comforted by the notion that the desert was where she belonged, that there were worse places to disappear.

As she ascended the rusty heap, the junkyard's occupants began to squawk in unison. Amy recognized their all too familiar announcement,

WE ARE NEARING MARS!
LANDING IS IMMINENT!

ALECTRYOMANCER

Rey could smell the gasoline used to set the pitch black horse on fire.

Not the first time he'd encountered this burning horse, this vision, if vision it was. Came and went, day or night. Sickening scene unfurling before his eyes with cruel predictability.

Others saw the horse too. Rey knew this, though they wouldn't admit to such. Kept their heads lowered. Scratched at the dirt. The meek refused to acknowledge this violation of their world.

Rey continued to hack at the packed soil with a short handled hoe. Thinning the lettuce, slowly moving down the rows. Acres of land extending to the base of the hills turned magenta by thickets of Chaparral Pea. All he could hear was the violent clamor of fire consuming that animal as it faded away in the direct light.

The sun beat down with such violence the horse became a cataract on the horizon. Rey knew better than to investigate; he'd done so several times before only to find nothing left behind. Not even a scorch mark on the ground.

He drank warm water from a canteen. There were fewer field hands working today. He turned his mind to more pressing matters. Just hours from now Little Cerefino would be fighting El Amarrador's gamecock. *Alectryomancer.*

Stuff of legend right there. The mysterious *El Amarrador* and his fierce stag *Alectryomancer.*

He swung the hoe, gouged out portions of an earth cracked into sloppy geometric patterns. Poorly defined hexagons a child-God has clumsily scrawled across the landscape.

Possibility of a strike had some in the camp fearing more violence. Talk of renewed vigilante attacks, like those against the CAWIU years back, was passed around. Four more laborers had disappeared in the last two days. Whether they'd abandoned the ranch to move on to other camps, headed back east, or met some criminal fate was unknown. Families came and went. Only the foreman seemed concerned about how many it'd been so far.

Rey sat in the shade of his tent. He pulled a JONATHAN CLUB cigar box from the center of a tightly rolled blanket. Opened the lid, removed the book inside, set it on the blanket. Carefully lifted a small stack of photographs and placed them on the book. He looked down at the gaffs inside. Curved blades and thin steel honed razor sharp. All neatly arranged. At the bottom of the box, beneath it all, a glass bottle labeled Isopropyl Alcohol Rubbing Compound was securely held in place by wads of cotton, to protect against breaking if jostled.

He randomly chose a photograph. Gently turned it over in his hands, luxuriated in the glossy texture. Only picture he had left of his son and two daughters. Lost the one of his wife years back in the fire.

Memory had become less reliable the longer he was away from home. Absent husband and father, past fading as he continued this grueling life of drudgery and toil. Hope for a reunion had become as rare as a can of peaches in sweet syrup. He slipped the picture into his shirt pocket, careful to keep dirt crusted hands from flaking onto the surface.

He removed another snapshot. Anything to distract himself from the omnipresent hunger. It was a beautiful field of sunflowers, taken long ago under circumstances no longer apparent. He did recall that he and his older brother used to play hide and seek here.

His brother would pocket a long piece of twine, loop it around a sunflower stalk, skulk as far away as the twine allowed, and then tug on it to make the plant's head bob and sway. The misdirection fooled Rey every time. Never knew he'd been tricked until his brother admitted it the night before he left home to join the 57th Infantry Regiment.

The photograph was a reminder of how happy he'd been back when everyone was alive and well. Poring over these pictures had become a ritual, a reassurance there'd been people he loved, a geography he'd once populated.

But these were false representations of his past. A picture of a pretty field of flowers didn't capture the pain of tearing his knee open on a rock that day, of dust in his eyes, the smell of the soil and sunflowers and the sound of insects in the air. These were just brief moments that didn't convey the struggle of poverty or the emptiness that populated those long stretches when a camera wasn't present.

There were times he feared God had changed history to suit some divine whim. If so, these snapshots must be part of His holy conspiracy.

This didn't sit well with Rey. Had little use for a God that laid out all the rules beforehand but refused to play fair. Preferred the vindictive petty tyrant in the older books of the Bible. That one was reliable. Allowed mankind their dalliances and punished accordingly.

Rey picked up the book. The burgundy cover was blank. Thin paper, like onion skin, yellowed, roughly cut edges. A journal of someone he'd known at some point? May have won it in a raffle. Maybe not. Perhaps he'd held onto it in hopes there was something within that could unlock the secrets of the burning horse. He no longer remembered.

Didn't know if he just forgot what he'd read every time he closed the pages, or if the words themselves bent into different shapes when he wasn't looking.

"You the man gonna fight Alectryomancer?" The boy stood just outside Rey's tent. Couldn't have been more than 8. Small even for his age, hair faded by the sun, vague familiarity to that tousled hair and set of his jaw. Wide eyes retained that vestige of innocence all children are born with and all God's creatures have absolved shortly thereafter.

"That's right. El Amarrador accept my wager?" Rey placed the field of sunflowers picture back on the stack.

"Yeah. He's ok with them odds. He said, 'Gambling gods ain't benevolent. Don't expect benevolence from no man neither.' That's what he said. El Amarrador is good for the cash."

Rey's smile fell into a grimace. He didn't appreciate being fooled by a little fool. "Real heavy plunger this *Amarrador.*" He laughed, humorless and harsh.

"Alectryomancer will kill that goddamn gamecock a yours."

Rey grabbed the boy's neck with such speed the kid didn't have time to gasp. Stuck a thumb under his eye. Pressed hard.

"Alectryomancer ain't ever been beat." The boy's words were defiant, but his voice quavered with fear.

"You go back to your papa or uncle or whatever he is to you and tell him he's fucking done."

"Ain't nothin' done 'til everything's burnt up." The boy gasped.

Rey ran his thumb across the boy's cheek, dirt under the nail leaving a line. Pressed against the tender throat.

He imagined this face mangled by fire.

"What are you goin' on about?"

"El Amarrador seen the black horse burn. I seen it too."

Shared visions. Something reached across the world. Spoke across vast distances from the confines of a void. Rey couldn't understand how this could be. He leaned his thumb deeper into the boy's neck.

"What an awful sight a that beautiful stallion. The smell and the awful sight." Kid cried slobbery hot tears now, moaned in terror. Pain caused him to pour his soul out—fear the contents of his bladder. "Stupid animal not even movin' a muscle. But I know it done stealed away people from these parts. Lifted them up in the air."

Rey didn't have the words to describe how the horse was more than a dumb animal; it was something eloquent that held the grandeur of the world in its grisly demise. Couldn't elaborate on the dread that accompanied its visit, the sense of inevitability, of futility in its every manifestation.

A portent of something incomprehensible.

Rey looked at the child with an expression that felt foreign on his skin.

"How do you know?"

The boy fell from his fearsome grasp, cringing in anticipation of a blow. "I just know."

"You and this *Amarrador* better not be tryin' to cold-deck me."

The boy ran. Disappeared somewhere between the jumble of gunnysacks and patchwork tents. Left a dark puddle in the dirt and the stink of scare-piss behind.

Rey didn't follow. His muscles ached from an accumulation of hours crouched in positions his body would never become accustomed. He sat on the pile of straw that served as a mattress, grateful he'd managed to procure a spot to sleep all alone. There'd been times he'd been forced to rent small bunkhouses with as many as 20 other men.

He wanted to stretch out and fall asleep but the *pelea de gallos* was soon. He listened to a fork scrape its tines against a tin plate, scattered snores of workers already sleeping. The black horse's frothy sweat and singed hair gasoline stench clung to his palate like grease. His stomach growled.

How could the boy have known? He pushed the cigar box aside, opened the book. Every time he cracked the spine he found himself discovering something never seen before.

He allowed it to fall open to a random page. It parted at a photograph he must've used as a bookmark at some point.

He studied the people in the snapshot, scrutinized the masks they wore. Knew nothing of its origins, no idea why they were dressed in such a manner. The child was familiar, but most children looked the same to him. There was something ominous in their demeanor, as if the camera had caught them in the act of a ceremony that necessitated disguising themselves. Identities obscured like his God's face.

He turned it over to find writing on the back:

Oh how I wish my children were near! I have always loved you, and though misfortunes necessitate a cruel benefactor, I remain [illegible smear of ink] *with love and eternal grace.*

Tempus edax rerum

It wasn't Rey's handwriting, though he felt as if he'd known the hand that had written it.

He put the bookmark aside and began reading.

NOACHIAN ANTEDILUVIAN ENGINES

Primates were hardwired to assist in the construction of Antediluvian Engines. Phainothropus further exploited these innate primate proclivities and applied a coefficient manifestation in the genetic substrate of primate brain's amenability to learning and manufacturing. (**McConnely, John.** Materials Resources and Engineering. Quantum Integrity, v. 6, issue 2).

Saltationist ("Yahwaptationist") advances amongst Phainothropus entities have not only been expressed as alien cognitions, per the vagaries of dualistic-hypotheses derived from mechanistic linear provocations, but also empirically demonstrated amongst proto-humans surpassing the viability of homo sapiens memory (**Inoue, Sana; Matsuzawa, Tetsuro.** Working memory of numerals in chimpanzees. Current Biology, v. 17, issue 23). There is a large body of work demonstrating extensive *Gorilla beringei* tool use in the wild, independent of Phainothropus interference (**Breuer, T., Ndoundou-Hockemba, M. and Fishlock, V.** First Observation of Tool Use in Wild Gorillas. PLoS Biol 3(11)). Primate brain function is much more pronounced than Phainothropus monistic inferences have implied, purporting the deducto-hypothetical stance that proto-humans were predisposed towards the menial tasks and slave labor required to construct Antediluvian Engines in deference to Deluge-Impacts (**Jarrod, Ignatius.** Towards a Mechanization of Antiquity. Origin Reports v. 4, issue 8).

The question of epistemic relativism, specifically as it relates to how a Noachic predecessor, aka *Phainothropus*, could communicate with primate entities or intelligences derived from esoterically-crystalline-Czochralski processes, is presented in confluence (**Kramer, Janice.** Integrae Naturae. Journal of Theo-syncretism, pp.488). A community comprised of Phainothropus entities most likely took up residence with proto-human colonies, proceeded to assimilate amongst the creatures, and then exploited their predilection towards engineering skills to build Antediluvian Engines in anticipation of the Flood.

The sun was rapidly setting. It was too dark to continue reading.

Rey held the book with limp hands.

A dreadful weight.

How could he have thought this nonsense had anything to do with those waking dreams of conflagrations and a horse that never died, just stood stock-still in the fields, blazing as if some internal engine churned hell in its gut? Maybe this book was a religious document, holy writ to remind him of the creeds he'd failed. Or those that had failed him.

He retained a dim memory of mingling with the I AM folks, with various Rizalista movements. Even ran with the Divine Order of the Royal Qarm of the Great Eleven, though he was certain he hadn't been involved in Willa Rhoads desecration way back when. He'd done things he wasn't proud of. Gave himself up to various faiths in hopes he'd discover that kernel of piety he'd known from his youth.

But the fire had changed everything.

After that tragedy he no longer worried much about God's opinions. The words in this book had nothing to do with what he'd been and who he was now.

He looked into the dusk as if darkness could purge his confusion. Phainothropus primates and Antediluvian Engines? Nonsense poetry and scientific bullshit.

So why couldn't he bring himself to get rid of the book?

He pulled an old yet functioning Gruen watch out of his trouser pocket. The dials were visible if he leaned into the setting sun's purple light dusting the camp.

Cockfight in less than an hour.

He placed a tattered Tyrolean straw hat on his head. Set the book back in the cigar box, on top of the photographs, gaffs and bottle below it all. Held the box under his left arm as if they were chocolates and he was off to a date. Walked past the poorly constructed bullpens and gunnysacks stretched between wood frames. So many vacant now.

He paused in front of a tent. A woman sat inside with a boy and two girls. Hunger made Rey curious as to what she was preparing. She pushed her tangled dirty hair over one shoulder, poured thick soup from a dented pot into a ceramic vase. Placed her hands on the side of the vase and turned it upside down.

A quivering rubbery cylinder slid out. Fetal shapes floated in the center of the cloudy upright mass, like developing chicks inside an egg.

The woman noticed Rey. Offered a warm smile. "Care to join us? There's plenty to go around."

The children looked up at him with soft gazes. Rey felt uneasy at what he'd seen. They began to aggressively poke at the jelly with their dirty hands.

Rey mumbled something noncommittal and walked away.

The chicken coops were kept at the perimeter of the camp—far enough away to allow some discretion despite the animal's crowing, near enough the contractors could keep an eye on them while allowing the men their recreational gambling.

Rey had sent money home to his wife and children over the years, but was too embarrassed to admit he'd been living in squalor. Never deluded himself into thinking he was a good man, but after all the fights and thieving and gambling he still held a certain pride in providing.

Lately even this had fallen to the wayside. Exorbitant debts and a drastic decrease in field labor wages saw to that. Only occasionally fooled with the four-bit broads, majority of his cash went to gambling and paying for his gamecock's upkeep.

He set the cigar box down. Removed the dirty undershirt draped over the cage to keep Little Cerefino from getting agitated on seeing other stags. Bird usually ate better than him: forty pellets every morning, handful of cooked grains, dose of lemon and sugar just to keep his insides clean. But there was no food inside the cage now. 24-hour fast made the bird a better fighter.

Little Cerefino was a white hackle cross, powerful, noble in his simplicity. A stupid beast whose sole purpose, if any purpose could be ascribed to any living thing, was to fuck and fight. Born and bred to satisfy the cockfighter's voracious appetite for sport and blood.

Rey held Little Cerefino in the crook of his elbow. Ran a finger across the smooth wattle and comb he'd expertly dubbed with a razor blade. Closed the cage, retrieved his box. Passed between the furrows on the dark scurfy fields in the direction of the distant hills.

A falling star cut a bright path across the sky.

Rey used to see strange things up there when he was younger. Called them "ancient-engines". Concocted all manner of stories about where the ancient-engines had come from. Gave gruesome descriptions of their epic battles and malign intent. A boy playing make-believe games of war.

The land was desolate. The distant scrub pines twisted wire miniatures in a child's diorama. Segments of sun bleached wood and rusted nails littered the ground—remnants of a *gallera's* construction. He passed by leather cords attached to spikes driven into the earth. One tether ended in a chaos of feathers and dried bones. Waste of a good meal there.

A clapboard structure occupied the center of the clearing. Nearby, several empty cock hutches sat silhouetted against the sky, stacked high atop each other, like strange desert growths. The subdued rumble of men talking and guff laughter came from the interior of the ramshackle *gallera.*

The gateman sat on a metal folding chair. Left peeper nothing but fatty tissue, like something a butcher planned on saving for his dogs after the day was done. Two men stood, one at his left, other at his right.

Tall one looked to be napping while standing, thumbs hooked into his faded overalls. Other pulled deeply from a poorly rolled cigarette. Stared up at the stars as if expecting more company to fall down.

Rey fought the urge to turn around to see if the burning horse was behind him.

The gateman's remaining eye glowed with a strange eagerness in the light cast by the trouble lamps hanging from hooks on the *gallera's* canvas walls. A generator growled from somewhere nearby, emitting gasoline fumes, acrid and persistent.

"You gonna need to be approachin' if you intend to enter these premises," the gateman said.

Rey touched the photograph in his pocket for reassurance. The gateman's sunburnt face added a severity to an expression that didn't reach the amusement on his lips. Wore spit shined Bluchers the color of a redbone hound. Ivory slacks looked to have been denied the attentions of an iron for quite some time.

"Fine *gallo*." The gateman ran a thumb and forefinger along his salt and pepper mustache drooping with sweat.

"Yes he is. Little Ceferino. A real pug." Rey smiled.

"You business in bein' here?"

"Fighting Alectryomancer tonight."

The smoker raised an eyebrow. Picked a flake of tobacco off his tongue.

The gateman leaned forward in his chair, hands on knees. Scrutinized Rey from dusty boots to battered hat. "El Amarrador's Alectryomancer? *Y su gallo negro?*"

Rey nervously tucked Little Ceferino under his other arm. Moved the cigar box to the other hand. "I have dough. Worked my way through the circuit."

"I know who the fuck you is. You and the bird. Real money bird."

"Six time champion. I'm on the level."

The gateman slapped his knee as if he'd just been told a solid joke. "Who needs Ham 'n' Eggs in their dotage when you got a nest egg in cockfightin'! Am I right boys?"

Neither the tall sleeper nor smoker responded.

"You know El Amarrador never been beat?" The gateman sounded incredulous.

Rey knew this. El Amarrador had quite the reputation in the pitting racket. Reputation outside as well. Said to have made and lost fortunes on tin and rubber in Singapore. Came home to rub shoulders with Silver Shirts at the Murphy Ranch. Renowned cockfighter had traveled far and wide. Dabbled in strange and disreputable new movements. All this been said and more.

But Rey had his own past to contend with. He was determined to win tonight.

"I have dough. Here to pit with El Amarrador's Alectryomancer," he repeated.

"We've gone over this already pally." The gateman turned his head, hocked a wad of yellow phlegm into the dirt. "You got the fee?"

"Entrants don't pay a fee."

"You're an exception pally." He held up five fingers on one hand, bent thumb and forefinger formed an O with the other.

"Never had to pay before."

"Well you sure as fuck is gonna this time."

"Goddamn frame-up." Rey handed over the 50-cent entrance charge. Could've picked up a cheap steak and a pack of Model cigarettes for that price. The tin was a bigger hit than he'd expected to pay.

"Referee'll be waitin' inside." The gateman paused before finishing with *pally*. He leaned back in his chair, surreptitiously slipped the coin into a pocket that jangled like a successful beggar's cup.

The smoker waved Rey through into the *gallera*. Tall sleeping man continued to do just that.

The pit was an oval space with a packed dirt floor, about 18-feet in diameter. The thigh-high barrier walls were built from rusty chicken wire and ragged pieces of wood lashed together with twine. Folding chairs surrounded the pit.

Folks had traveled far to be here; there were men from various camps within a 50-mile radius. Some gamblers sat, others stood. The shorter ones in the back did so on wooden fruit crates.

Rey recognized the referee from a bout he'd attended in Santa Barbara earlier in the year. A good man, well trusted. Known to be scrupulously fair when it came to his avocation.

El Amarrador squatted in the center of the pit. He held Alectryomancer wedged between his knees, like a farrier grasping a skittish stud's hoof as he hammered the shoe in position. Swiped a big hand across Alectryomancer's soot-black trimmed feathers. Rey had never seen such an animal before. Jet-black, beak and all.

El Amarrador met Rey's gaze. Eyes all pupil, dark as the rooster's feathers. Face smooth as a razor strop, like stubble had never marred its surface. He'd met this man before, was certain of it. Couldn't describe the circumstances.

The referee held a Standing Liberty between thumb and forefinger. "Call it gentlemen."

El Amarrador stood, looked down from a great height. "You first."

"Heads," Rey said.

The coin flashed like a diamond in the air, fell onto the referee's open hand. "We have the Lady! Short or long?"

"Short." Rey opened his cigar box. Carefully set the photographs and book aside. Removed the stubby sharp spurs and patches of chamois hole-punched in the center. Slipped them onto Little Cerefino's leg, over the area where his natural spurs had been dubbed. Splashed liquid from the isopropyl bottle onto a wad of cotton. Wiped the gaffs, leg, and talons clean.

He tied the metal spur on. Looped the wax string several times so the thin blade would stay securely attached to the leg. Did this to both legs, cock scratching and fussing all the while. Rey looked over his shoulder and saw El Amarrador was ready with Alectryomancer.

"Time limit or kill?" the referee asked.

Rey looked to El Amarrador. The large man just smiled.

"Kill," Rey spoke on his behalf.

The crowd was as agitated as a stallion smelling a mare in heat.

Finger betting began. Low roar of shouted numbers, extending one finger, five, back and forth. Money passed between work worn hands.

The referee wiped a wet cotton ball across Little Cerefino's spurs to remove any traces of poison or noxious substances—professional cockfighter wouldn't dream of pulling that particular grift, but rules were rules. He forced Little Cerefino's beak open, squeezed the excess water from the cotton into his mouth. Satisfied the bird hadn't been peppered or soaped, he turned to El Amarrador.

The large man lifted Alectryomancer above his head. Held him up like a newly acquired trophy. The crowd broke into a chant.

Alectryomancer! Alectryomancer! Alectryomancer!

The referee wiped down the black bird. Blew against the feathers, exposed the dark skin underneath. Finished, he stepped to the side of the pit, shaking his head at El Amarrador's antics. He waved his hat in the air to get the crowd's attention.

"Little Ceferino versus Alectryomancer! No time limit! Short gaffs! Gamecocks weigh in at 4 pounds each! *Enoro!*"

Rey pressed a palm against the snapshot in his pocket. Tried to imagine what his daughter's faces looked like, the way his son held his hands to his mouth while sleeping. How their voices might sound if he'd enough details to conjure them up once more.

He gave a silent prayer to his children.

His wife.

His God.

"Bill your cocks!" the referee shouted.

They held their gamecocks out at arm's length. The stags fussed. Clawed and pecked. Rage sparking their instinct to kill. Puffed up twice their size. Alectryomancer's obsidian plumage glowed a purple tint in that light.

The two men crouched, each on their side of the chalk lines. One hand clasped against their cock's breast, other clutching tail feathers.

The referee nodded. "Pit 'em!"

They released their gamecocks.

Little Cerefino leapt into battle as if he had a hot pepper up his ass and came down hard on Alectryomancer's back. Spur parted feathers, bit into the stag's dark skin.

Alectryomancer rolled away. Fluttered dust off his feathers. A strange nightmare thing all bristled with aggression. A spider with feathers.

He ran at Little Cerefino, thin legs a blur, chest held forward. Pecked at his opponent's head like a trained *piqueros*. Dazed him, flipped back talons up and sank spurs into Little Cerefino's breast.

A point was so deeply lodged Alectryomancer had to bounce on one leg as he struggled to withdraw the gaff.

"Handle!" the referee commanded.

The cockfighters pulled their bird's apart. Retreated to their respective sides of the chalk lines.

Alectryomancer's blood was black as motor oil. El Amarrador's hands glistened dark and wet.

Rey pressed his thumb against the hole in Little Cerefino's chest until the bleeding slowed. He was already in a bad way. Despite all the black blood it looked like Alectryomancer was fine. That demon bird's wound was all show but no blow.

"Pit!"

The cocks rushed at each other, wings outstretched. Dark outline of Alectryomancer contrasted against the filthy whitewashed pit walls like a mythical creature from a stone carving.

Little Cerefino tried another aerial attack, but that dark bird was too fast. He took advantage of the opening, jabbed at Little Cerefino's head with both spurs slitting feathers and skin. Lacerated the cock's eyeball. Jelly gushed down his beak.

Everyone in the noisy confinement of that gallera heard the impact. Little Cerefino was bleeding something awful from his eyehole.

"Handle!"

Rey took Little Cerefino's head in his mouth, sucked the excess blood and eyeball mush from the empty socket.

Nothing to be done about it. Cock was blind on one side now.

He spit the bird's hot blood into the dirt. Worked up some fresh saliva, spat into Little Cerefino's mouth. Rubbed him warm. Held his finger against the breast wound even though it had already grown a tacky layer. "Not yet Cerefino. Not yet."

Any hope of a win was fading fast.

The cocks flew at each other. Sleek killers, one a beautiful rusty orange and metallic green, the other otherworldly. Black as space.

Alectryomancer had the upper hand each pit, battering and slicing Little Cerefino, yet refraining from the final strike. Tiny feathers floated in the air.

By the fourth pitting it looked like all was lost. If Rey didn't know any better he'd say Alectryomancer was intentionally prolonging the match, as if some predetermined amount of time had to pass before he could vanquish his foe.

Alectryomancer broke Little Cerefino's left wing seconds into the fifth pitting. Even hobbled, wing dragging uselessly through the dirt, he was still a gallant bird as fury propelled him into combat, determined to hang a heel.

Alectryomancer rushed Little Cerefino. Lifted a few inches into the air, sailed down low, spurs extended for the kill. Little Cerefino gave a pathetic but valiant hop in an attempt to defend himself, but his left wing held him back. His injury forced him into a spin that threw Alectryomancer's trajectory off.

The black rooster hit the dirt hard.

Little Cerefino continued moving, spurs swinging in an arc. One sank into Alectryomancer's neck, other pierced his eye and slid into the brain with the sound of an icepick stabbing slushy ice.

Alectryomancer fell over limp and lifeless.

Those who'd taken a risk in betting on Little Cerefino howled with success. Most of the crowd spat *cabron!* at the gamecock and his handler.

The earth trembled.

A few laughed at the surprise, made jokes about the earthquake's timing. The rest waited it out with grim determination. Trouble lamps swayed for a full two-minutes after the aftershocks subsided.

Rey restrained Little Cerefino under his armpit. Poured cold water over his feathers, washed him up best he could. Wiped down the gaffs nice and neat. Stored them back in the cigar box beneath the book and photographs.

El Amarrador stood over Alectryomancer. Flies had already started to land on the *verga*. The big man's shoulders shook as he sobbed.

He lifted Alectryomancer with such reverence you'd expect him to have blessed the little corpse right then and there.

But he just stood in silence, shirt and arms so wet with blood Rey could smell it as far away as he was. Odor made him think of fire and that black horse.

Gamblers slapped Rey on the back. Drunk faces cheered him on. A fistfight broke out near the back of the *gallera*.

El Amarrador turned to Rey. Didn't seem to care much that his tears left trails on his dusty skin. Kind of man that wore his emotions on his sleeve and wouldn't think twice to correct your error at drawing attention to it. He solemnly shook Rey's hand.

"Regular *navajeros* that gamecock a yours. Don't know how he did it."

"Fair fight." Rey wiped black blood on his trousers.

"Alectryomancer never lost a bout."

"What kind a bird is that?"

"Not from these parts. One of a kind really."

"Never seen the likes."

"Wasn't supposed to happen like that. No telling what machinery been set in motion now."

"What about my money?"

"Get it tomorrow. The boy will fetch it."

"You don't have it?"

"I do not."

"Suppose I got no choice."

"None whatsoever. Like that little tremor we got right before that earthquake. Metal orbs shifting under our feet. Can't control none of it."

"Don't know any a that from nothin'." A spasm rippled down Rey's neck. Those words were familiar.

El Amarrador placed his thick hand on Rey's shoulder. Little Cerefino squawked. "Incomprehensible machines evolving beneath our feet. At the mercy of time."

"A preacher and a cockfighter! Don't recognize the verse."

"Not much use for scripture."

"I've seen 'em gambling."

"What's that?"

"Preachers. Even knew one was a priest by day, referee by night. Only talked about Revelations and the Baby Jesus and *vaqueros* with a scale in each hand."

"No use for that talk either." El Amarrador paused, looked down at the dead rooster in his arms. "Wanderin' a landscape already been written."

"Gambling makes you question how things come about the ways they did."

El Amarrador shook his head. "What's the use if the Engine makes it so all is bound to happen the way it does?"

El Amarrador was drunk. He was a teller of tall tales, his words a drunkard's philosophy. Rey had dealt with men like this before. Braggarts. Liars.

These were the best moments anyone here would ever experience. Life would never be better than when the bird they'd placed money on struck down an opponent.

Most labor camps were segregated. Hapas, Mexicans, and whites occupied their own place, *los mas moreno, lo mas pobre.* But ethnic divisions were trivial when it came to gambling. Were they not all nothing but stoop laborers and pea pickers and fruit tramps destined to throw wages at floating taxi dances, raffles and lotteries? Gamble on death in hopes they'd achieve some sort of grandeur beyond the grime and the sweat? All of God's children.

Rey had accepted that his God was no longer the traditional one with all the pomp that came with the faith he'd been born into. These days his God was a dusty fur-clad thing, dispersing life about the land as if all of His creatures were trample-burs shed from holy garb. Rey's Lord wore the armor of the mountains and deserts, went into battle with a face disguised by cold blue skies. A clandestine, inscrutable God.

"I'll get my dough tomorrow?"

El Amarrador made eye contact, gaze locked in place as if Rey was lined up in a rifle's fixed point sight. "I know why folks been disappearin' from the camps."

"Disappearing?"

"Government been abducting folks."

"Like Canete's camp? You tell a lot of strange tales. Like your boy."

"He been talkin'?"

"Talked about a burned up horse takin' people into the heavens."

"Boys play cruel games. Burn snakes and lizards. Boys tell stories."

Rey detected something beneath the words. El Amarrador wasn't a skilled liar.

But he didn't pursue the matter. Didn't think the infamous cockfighter even had the means to answer anyhow. He thought to bring up one more issue before leaving.

"I get the sense we met before."

El Amarrador didn't acknowledge the comment, just looked at his dead bird and mumbled, "You've set something in motion that shoulda been left alone."

"How's that?" Rey asked.

But El Amarrador just kept up with slipping his hand across

Alectryomancer's smooth black feathers.

It was evident any and all talk was done.

Little Cerefino died on the way back to camp. Rey put him back in the coop. He'd bury him in the morning.

He ate the last remaining grapefruit to still his stomach cramps. Drank some water. Lit a lantern, picked out a photograph from the cigar box. It was a snapshot of a kitchen.

Someone else's memories.

This struck him as so fanciful it frightened him. Were he and his wife not relieved when the running water had finally been installed out there in the middle of the countryside where they'd raised their son and daughters? Was it not here, sitting at that very table, that their daughter ran in to tell them about the terrible fire?

He was sure of it, though nothing was certain anymore.

He put the picture away and read from the book.

SHRIEK'D AGAINST HIS CREED

I attest that Darwin plagiarized from Robert Chambers (Vestiges of the Natural History of Creation, 1844), Patrick Matthew (On Naval Timber and Arboriculture, 1831), and his grandfather Erasmus Darwin (Zoonomia, 1794) in an attempt to substantiate his central thesis that "we are descended from barbarians" (The Descent of Man, p. 796). Darwin perpetrated this fraud so as to substantiate a non-Euclidean fact(less)-space with which to dogmatize (i.e., desensitization of primal neo-cortic paradigms) his core beliefs.

Darwin's zeal to label human origins as animalistic was a plot to obviate his murderous nature, to obscure his own crimes—specifically his murdering his two firstborn children (conveniently recorded as being stillborn) and his subsequent lapse into depravity. Darwin's voyage on the Beagle was his attempt to portray other cultures as cannibals, to justify his abnormal appetites (**Strauss, Clara.** Psycho-analysis and the Enfeebled Victorian Mind, 1902, p. 325).

Darwin compared the native 'del Fuegans to sub-humans and denigrated them mercilessly: "I could not have believed how wide was the difference between savage and civilised man: it is greater than between a wild and domesticated animal, inasmuch as in man there is a greater power of improvement." (The Voyage of the Beagle, p. 103)

"These poor wretches were stunted in their growth, their hideous faces bedaubed with white paint, their skins filthy and greasy, their hair entangled, their voices discordant and their gestures violent. Viewing such men, one can hardly make oneself believe that they are fellow-creatures, and inhabitants of the same world. It is a common subject of conjecture what pleasure in life some of the lower animals can enjoy: how much more reasonably the same question may be asked of these barbarians! At night... [they] sleep on the wet ground coiled up like animals." (The Voyage of the Beagle, p. 104)

"These Fuegians are Cannibals; but we have good reason to suppose it carried on to an extent which hitherto has been unheard of in the world." (personal letter from Darwin to C.S. Darwin, 1833)

Darwin was even cruel in his amusement at observing the "savages". He mocked them in a letter dated May 23, 1833, to his cousin, "In Tierra del [sic] I first saw bona fide savages; & they are as savage as the most curious person would desire. A wild man is indeed a miserable animal, but one well worth seeing."

Darwin even made jest concerning the assassination of Fuegians in a letter to C.T. Whitley, "... to day I ordered a Rifle & 2 pair of pistols; for we shall have plenty of fighting with those d—— Cannibals: It would be something to shoot the King of the Cannibals Islands."

Whitley, disturbed at Darwin's atavistic descent, wrote back, "I will not disturb your "ordering" occupations or your cannibal shooting..."

This dehumanization of the natives justified Darwin's equating them with animals. This exacerbated his initial foray into violence when he murdered a native child and devoured the boy's fatty tissues in a sado-erotic manifestation of ritualistic hubris.

A coyote yipped somewhere near the hills. Didn't sound like any coyote heard before.

Rey fell asleep.

The smoldering horse visited late that night. Shone with such fervor he awoke several times expecting to be met by the rising sun. In the morning he went to bury Little Cerefino, but something had broken into the coop and snatched away the carcass.

The sun angered up Rey's daydreams vivid and rough.

A rusty shadow approached. Rey leaned on his hoe, adjusted his hat to better protect his eyes from the glare. Though it wasn't the horse vision this shape *did* move with the gait of a wounded animal. Loping, limbs not working in conjunction.

The creature kept at it. Clomping forward as if its feet were too heavy. Waves of heat squiggled from the ground like ethereal snakes.

Rey looked up just in time to find a tawny bundle of rags bearing down. El Amarrador's boy knocked the hoe from his hands.

Rey clambered to his feet. The boy crawled on all fours with such ferocity he thought it might be an animal dressed up in a child's clothes. One of them *aswang* some told tales about when they were feeling particularly nostalgic and superstitious.

"What the hell got into you?" He grabbed the boy's arm, hauled him upright.

The child was even thinner than before. Feral quality to a mouth set crooked by missing or distorted teeth. Eyes collapsed deeper and darker, dead moons never graced by starlight. At first Rey thought the boy's skin was charred black, then the odor hit him and he realized he was caked in dried excrement. An animal. No longer familiar.

"You got my money?"

The boy lunged, bit down hard, teeth scraping out a furrow on the back of Rey's hand.

He kicked the child in the chest. Felt a thin bone snap underfoot. Boy fell flat on his ass.

"Little fucking bastard!" Moved forward to kick him again.

The boy quickly sprang to his feet despite his cracked ribs. Moved so fast he was a speck in the distance by the time Rey caught enough breath to pursue.

Nobody working in the field seemed to notice any of this. If they did they didn't acknowledge it.

Rey's hand turned red and puffy like an overfilled hot water bottle. The wound was ragged and filthy. He'd see to it that El Amarrador pay what was owed. Provide what was his. See to it that his brat got punished too.

He worked until the sun dipped behind the hills. There were no cockfights that evening. Word had spread that the Sheriff had raided the pit. Labor contractor was gathering the necessary funds for a bribe to resume the fights. He'd have to go tomorrow, follow up on El Amarrador and his money. Teach that boy respect.

Days ago he'd used the last of his funds to pick up some meager provisions. Ate a heap of fried potatoes. Drank some strong coffee. Scoured the skillet with handfuls of sand. Left it outside in the night air to cool down. His hand ached something terrible.

Later that evening strange sounds came from the tent near his but he didn't go explore. Couldn't explain why, but the last thing he wanted to find were those very same children greedily digging into their gelatinous meal.

Rey worked through the morning. Had yet to hear any talk on whether the cockfights were on again. He was going tonight anyway. *Gallera* was the only place El Amarrador might be found. Shortly after sunset he wrapped the book in his jacket and buried the bundle underneath the straw.

He could remember some of the book now. Lengthy passages built up in his head like the nest of a cactus wren in a cholla plant. Cannibals and Phainothropus ran through his brain.

He wrapped his wounded hand with the old shirt he'd used to cover Little Cerefino's cage. The bite-mark was seeping clear fluid.

He needed to block out those words from the book. He looked at his straw bed and saw that a snapshot had fallen from the cigar box. It was a picture of the coffins.

He dwelled on the memory of the coffin maker. On the children's caskets and the coffin maker's camera. Rolled them over and over in his mind until they were worn slick like a pebble in a river.

He couldn't have been older than 7. The carpenter's business had prospered in the days after the fire. Despite the grim occasion the craftsman had spent some of his newly acquired wealth on a camera. Rey was so fascinated by the man's skill he'd asked for a photograph to document his handiwork. A memento, something he could show his brother. The carpenter had been happy to oblige as he knew Rey's parents and knew their boy was curious about the coffins.

That day came back, clear as a bell.

The smell of sawdust, shellac and linseed oil. Skies filled with smoke rising from the smoldering structures days after the fires had been put out.

That had been the day the ancient-engines paced Rey from the heavens. Followed him all the way down the path until he ran so fast he was able to lose them in the trees just before reaching home.

He remembered his heavy heart, a rebuke from his mother for making up stories about ancient-engines on such a tragic time when so many had died.

Rey stared at that little coffin and remembered the blackened skin of the victims cracked like dry soil, pink muscle visible in the lines. He hid the photograph under the straw.

Headed out across the fields to the barren area where he'd beaten Alectryomancer. The night was unusually quiet. A half moon offered a feeble light to walk by.

The *gallera* was no longer there. The stakes in the ground, leather cords, chicken bones—everything had vanished. He looked across the flat expanse.

Three figures stood in a loose circle around a metal trash can, sides glowing the color of an overripe tangerine. Sparks dribbled out of the can's mouth into the night.

Rey recognized the gatekeeper, the smoker, and the tall sleeper from the other night. Rugged men. Grifters eking a living from the gullible and vulnerable. Clothes dusted with travel.

"Where's the *gallera?*" Rey stepped within the trash can's light.

The gatekeeper was startled by the sudden appearance. "What we got here?"

The sleeper awoke. He leaned forward and grabbed Rey's arm. Twisted it behind his back. Pressed the flat edge of a knife against his cheek.

"No need for that!" Rey pulled away from the tall man.

Inexplicably, with no warning, they began to punch and kick.

Boots hit like mallets. They used fists then switched to whipping Rey with leather belts when their hands became too sore. Split skin stung like a serpent's nip.

Rey fell, stirred up talcum soft dust that enveloped them like fog. He kicked out but only hit air. Grabbed the pant leg of someone. Crusted wound on his hand split and burned as if he'd been branded. He lost his grip.

"You know me! You fucking know me! Why you killin' me?"

The gatekeeper looked down with his gloating eye. Observed Rey as if he'd found a lizard basking in the sun, listless, wondering if he should stamp it out or allow it to continue living. "Don't know who the fuck you is."

"What happened to the *gallera?*" Rey yelled over and over until the gatekeeper's heel struck his mouth and it became difficult to speak through the thick blood.

Rey prayed he'd look up and see the black horse. Maybe then

these men would sense that instinctive panic the animal invoked. Maybe they would catch its musk wafting this way, stench of blackened muscles making water in mouths like some crass miracle.

Maybe their seeing it would definitively prove that the horse was a real flesh and fire thing and not some phantom.

But the night refused to assist him.

Rey glared at the men through an eye that hadn't swollen shut. Couldn't describe how he looked to them. Brute existence filled him with terrible thoughts.

"Where's El Amarrador?" Red flecks from his lips spackled the pale dust.

The three men pulled strange fearful expressions at hearing that name. Their faces wobbled in the night like ash ejected from the blazing trash can.

"El Amarrador," Rey demanded again.

The men slowly retreated. Rey could only crouch there in agony, watch them pace backwards until their forms wavered. Minutes passed then they dissipated in the waning light like ghosts.

Rey slowly trudged back towards camp against a sky as colorful as neon lights in the city at night. The ochre hills were a dull glaze in contrast. He checked his shirt pocket to reassure himself that the snapshot was still safe and sound.

He stopped before a massive saguaro cactus.

Hadn't been here yesterday.

A majestic sight. Patience of nature, roots buried under sand, decades of waiting for that rare shower to nourish it. Thriving slowly but inexorably.

A cactus this size took over a century to reach such heights.

A century or more.

Club-like arms branched off in several directions, thickly spined and heavy with fruit. The sky gave off a strange light.

Rey was suddenly overwhelmed by an insatiable hunger. Nothing mattered save devouring the dripping fibers of that plant, to swallow his fill then continue greedily consuming until he emptied the contents of his stomach to make room for more.

His fingers slid into the cactus. Spines tore at his skin. He made a fist, withdrew clumps of pulp, spongy and clear. He ignored the small dark embryos floating in the handfuls of plant jelly he raised to his mouth. Honey thick fluids flowed down his chin.

He consumed until the cactus' wine-like juices intoxicated him. Dug deeper into that cactus, clawing towards an elusive pulse deep within, striving towards that plant's heart but found a leathery womb instead and marveled at how none of this was possible.

He tore the tissues away to reveal a human fetus inside.

He held it cupped in both hands. Leg and arm buds still soft, malleable even. The desert night air steamed off of its warm mass. The umbilical was a lumpy gray rope trailing deep inside the cactus. Rey bit the cord in two.

Oh I will die here, Rey thought. I will die standing, my body continuing its motion of swinging the hoe, relentless in its performance, corpse moving diligently in death in the only manner it has ever known.

That unnatural hunger got the better of him again. Every moral fibre within Rey's soul pleaded with him to stop, to reject his blasphemous thoughts. But he was weak and resumed his violation of the flesh, wallowed in his depravity.

He ate the fetus with gusto. He was now fully resigned to his descent into an amoral existence. Ate until his stomach cramped, vomited, and then succumbed to that preternatural appetite once more. He feasted late into the night.

Hours later he managed to find his way home.

The flavors remained cloyingly sweet on his tongue. He opened the book, but couldn't be sure whether what he read, or even whether the wicked deeds he'd committed were imagined or not.

PHAINOTHROPUS

Phainothropus energies as communicated from mediums both diffuse and antecedent to the chemical waveform of ontological substrates vis-à-vis the hyper awareness of an entity's comprehension. The neuro-aggregate of which one's existence is layered in multiple personalities as decreed by compatabilitist ideologies, or conversely, philosophies sympathetic to Molinism, to arrive at a new species. I have dubbed this being *Phainothropus.*

As distinct an entity, a separate person entombed within the DNA of an organism, yet, paradoxically, co-existing as a passenger despite their innate and profound connection(s). What consequences or choices is one given beneath such confining Mytho-poetic variables?

As such, if one can place the individual as I, postulating the person as occupying a space in time A), removed from said observation, repopulated to another point X distance away. As said heuristic argument is thus derived, the observer-receiver ration may be extrapolated from the Planck constant.

The coordinates of Phainothropus' severed head lie submerged just beneath the Mohorovičić discontinuity. It is suspected to have evolved from crystalline substrates, recalibrated fractal connections within cognitive clouds drifting from planet to planet, accumulating minerals to repopulate, rebuild, reconstruct, and reproduce. Perpetually. Of this comes the dawn of the new intelligence. The birth of Phainothropus.

This decapitated Phainothropus retains such power even in death; brain continuously transmitting an array of magnetic resonances. Its aura radiates far beyond the Earth's crust, into the cosmos, spreading units of contact across planets, focal points, ascribing ley lines of derivative neo-axiomatic postulates on Earth's continents, photovoltaic vitalization reaching an apex in the Afar Triangle region.

As such, these energies have influenced Homo sapiens' evolution. Atavistic reminders of heritage remain through bio mineralization, the presence of ferromagnetic materials in the brain and meninges tissues from Homo sapiens have revealed diamagnetic and paramagnetic conditions (**Kirschvink, J.** Magnetite biomineralization in the human brain. Proc. Natl. Acad. Sci., Vol. 89, pp. 7683-7687). Clear antecedents of biological consequences per Phainothropus' influence(s).

This Phainothropus head remains interred within the Earth's inner core, surrounded by nested spheres of various alloys, the most prevalent being a 1200k thick layer of iron. Phainothropus has surgically implanted a series of tubules between these layers, inserting a cerebro-spinal substance to accentuate the conductivity to aid in generating the electro-magnetic processes necessitating its generative occult manifestations. This inner core rotates at a greater speed than the other layers, which not only creates the Earth's magnetic field, but extends the field over the entirety of the planet's surface.

These energies are exacerbated by the internal heat generated in the mantle where convective cells circulate and power the processes from Phainothropus' brain that much more effectively. When operational, this Phainothropus organic device distorts space-time, thus instigating a singularity where the aether is altered by gravitational forces creating the perpetual feedback loop between infinite expansion and infinite contraction of the universe where consciousness as bound to time in a fixed point is no longer valid but becomes amendable to manipulation. The ability to traverse these barriers of time by the artificially created Phainothropic consciousness and the temporality achieved in such states delivers photon-tachyon particles which collide at the temporal luxon/bradyon barrier and propagate the permeability of tachyonic antitelephone mitigated time.

Rey burned the book the next morning.

Washed the stiff mask of blood from his face. Fried some side-meat in a skillet. Warmed a pot of bitter coffee with the vestiges of heat from the ash. The thick brew helped him sober up.

The foreman showed shortly after he'd finished eating.

"Didn't sleep much last night. Racket in the skies." The foreman held his hat in both hands like a soldier delivering bad news to a widow.

He continued when Rey didn't respond, "Down five more workers. Up and left last night I suppose. Not sure who's available no more."

Rey couldn't place the man. Vaguely familiar voice, like the tone of a schoolmate's idle chat he hadn't thought of in decades. "I ain't goin' nowhere. Need to work."

"Can you work? You look like you been beat."

"I need to work." His hand wound was oozing a clear jelly flecked with specks of an embryonic aspect. He wrapped the dirty shirt around the bite. Set the cup and plate down. Slipped his boots on.

Rey swung the serrated blade.

Lopped the lettuce free in neat strokes. Gathered the heads in a crate. His wounded hand dripped onto the dirt. Thick liquid *drip drip dripping* of seeds scattered across the soil.

He didn't recognize the few remaining field hands. They weren't speaking English or Spanish or Tagalog. Their voices were discordant and their gestures violent. As if they were finger betting at a match.

He watched ancient-engines crawl on the air like thin-legged insects over a scummy film grown across a stagnant pond. The machines were just as impressive as he'd remembered. He stuck a finger in his shirt pocket to make sure the photograph of his children was still there.

The pocket was empty.

He frantically looked up and down the rows. He held his reeling head and screamed down at the earth. Shouted out for that photograph as if it was a lost pet or a lost child and he didn't want to remember all those burnt little bodies. He raised his gaze.

The black horse was standing in the distance. It wasn't on fire anymore. It had never been this close before.

He could now see it wasn't an animal. Intricate parts moved like muscles under its skin. The flaming mane and tail were flickering lights streaming along cables. Some unfathomable internal combustion engine rumbled inside that mechanized steed. Stink of ethanol fumes spread out across the fields.

That horse-like contraption waited there unmoving. An ancient statue carved from onyx by a people forgotten to time. Rey couldn't understand how something so majestic, so complex with its inscrutable inner workings, could eventually be reduced to charred remains. The inexorable erosion of form and memory and hope.

Phainothropus sat upright on the horse apparatus.

It observed the world with passive indifference, its flesh as resplendent as the walls protecting the cities of Cibola. The air cracked into desiccated geometric segments.

Rey fell to the earth, scrabbled at the dirt in a desperate search for the photograph. The bright air burned so fervently he forced his mouth into the cool soil, mud clumping to lips parched from the sun. That cold refreshing earth shuddered beneath him. His wounded hand burned as if fiery worms were burrowing through the muscle.

Oh so many little blackened hands and feet.

Someone poured water over his head. Pressed a canteen between his shaking hands, his fingers were brittle and hard like pottery.

His hat had fallen off. He held his face in shaking calloused hands to protect his eyes from the terrible heat. He peeked between dirt stiff fingers.

He saw the photograph. Kneeled down to pick it up.

The pandemonium of the sun gripped him with such violence the ground cracked the air shook the firmament cracked wide in a trembling fit.

Nested metal spheres inside the earth spun. Phainothropus' severed head screamed electromagnetic waves. There was only a young girl in the picture. The faded figure behind her was unknown. Rey didn't recognize anyone in the photograph.

A terrible conflagration poured forth to scour the land in the ravages of time.

ABOUT THE AUTHOR

Christopher Slatsky is an author of weird fiction whose works have appeared in the anthologies *Arcane, Resonator: New Lovecraftian Tales From Beyond*, and the forthcoming *Summer of Lovecraft*. His stories have been published in *The Lovecraft eZine, Innsmouth Magazine, Xnoybis*, and several Dunhams Manor Press titles. He currently lives in the Los Angeles area.

DUNHAMS MANOR BOOKS
Est. 2013

DUN-01
THE CHOIR OF BEASTS
Nicole Cushing

DUN-02
THE YELLOW HOUSE
DJ Tyrer

DUN-03
NIGHTMARES FROM A LOVECRAFTIAN MIND
Jordan Krall

DUN-04
UNDER THE SHANGHAI TUNNELS
Lee Widener

DUN-05
A LIFE IN ANOTHER DREAM
Suresh Subramanian

DUN-06
THE BAD OUTER SPACE
Scott Nicolay

DUN-07
JESTER OF YELLOW DAY
W.H. Pugmire

DUN-08
THE MISSION
T.E. Grau

DUN-09
CHILDREN OF LIGHT
Daniel Mills

DUN-10
FAR FROM STREETS
Michael Griffin

COMING SOON:

PASSAGE TO THE DREAMTIME
Anya Martin

THE FACTS IN THE CASE OF CLARISSA COLLYER
Selena Chambers

XNOYBIS ISSUE TWO
Jordan Krall (ed.)

GORGONAEON
Jordan Krall

WICKER MEN SEMINARY BULLETIN
Jordan Krall (ed.)
Newsletter Only Available to WMS members

THE CASTLE-TOWN TRAGEDY
Brandon Barrows

JACK WERRETT, THE FLOOD MAN
Rebecca Lloyd

MUSCADINES
S.P. Miskowski

THE SECRET OF VENTRILOQUISM
Jon Padgett

THE STAY AWAKE MEN
Matthew Bartlett

MAPPING THE DARKNESS
Shawn Mann

IN PRAISE OF PAN
Jordan Krall (ed.)

A CHAMBER OF SLEEP
Jayaprakash Sathyamurthy

Printed in Great Britain
by Amazon